The Double

An Investigation

Fictions of Don Webb

TheDoubleTheDoubleTheDoubl
TheDoubleTheDoubleTheDoubl
TheDoubleTheDoubleTheDoubl
TheDoubleTheDoubleTheDoubl
TheDoubleTheDoubleTheDoubl
TheDoubleTheDoubleTheDoubl
TheDoubleTheDoubleTheDoubl
TheDoubleTheDoubleTheDoubl
TheDoubleTheDoubleTheDoub

Don Webb

St. Martin's Press ✠ New York

The Double

An Investigation

Design by Michaelann Zimmerman

Edited by Gordon Van Gelder

ISBN 0-312-19144-8

First edition: October 1998

10   9   8   7   6   5   4   3   2   1

To S. **Edred Flowers** and Thomas Pynchon, Uncle River and Stanley Marsh 3, Wendy Walker and Tom LaForge, E. Gary Gygax and Rosemary—whom I met in the Ultimate West, and to all called Sâlik, this Musâmarah, this Night Talk.

The Brotherhood of Travelers cannot confirm nor deny the superstition that if this book is carried with you it protects you from accidents of travel whether by car, by boat, by airplane, or by Thought alone.

Table of Contents

1 Do You Want to Dance?

John Reynman was six foot four inches tall, had blond hair that his ex-wife's pale dark hands had loved to caress into ingots, and eyes a rare steel gray. He had two tattoos, a logo for a rock band called the Electric Luddites on his left forearm (an embarrassing reminder of an acid trip in 1984), the other a black rose over his heart. He wore plain black-rimmed glasses. In short he looked just like the murdered man (except that his skull was intact) that lay on the parquet floor of his Austin home.

John knew that today wasn't going to be like any other day of the rest of his life. Just last night he had thrown a coin in a fountain and wished for excitement. For something uncanny.

Corpses smell. The newly shot in particular give off a steamy odor, a coppery smell for the blood, a sweet smell for the brains. John wanted to open the windows and get rid of the smell, but decided that for a few minutes he might keep the knowledge of the body before him a secret. He closed the front door.

There was a strange car in front of his house, a papyrus

white Mercedes-Benz 220 SE. Maybe the corpse had ridden here in it.

John sat down on his couch and pondered what to do.

Calling the police was the logical step, but it did seem a little awkward: "Excuse me, but there's a corpse in my house that looks a whole lot like me, it's been shot, could you come by and pick it up? No I have no idea who he was, or why he's here. I slept late today."

Hiding the body seemed a bit awkward as well.

Whoever had shot the body might want to return.

Perhaps they wanted to kill John. After all, this fellow was a dead ringer.

John laughed a little, a bit too high and fast.

He would figure out a little of what was going on. *Then* he would call the police.

Someone started the Mercedes outside and drove away. John went to the window, too late to get a clear view of the plates. Of course the Mercedes need have nothing to do with it, but you tend to associate new things with new things. His neighbor across the street, newly fired from his job at TekTron, was staring at him. He waved and the neighbor waved back.

He went back to the couch and rehearsed his speech to the police.

"I am a freelance game designer. I mainly write the text parts of computer game design. You know like *Sethos 1* or *Ulthar!* So I can pretty much keep my own hours. I slept late today. I didn't get up till nine o'clock, when I heard the postman delivering my mail. I came in the front room to pick up my mail. The first thing I noticed was the door was partially open, and while I was fussing with myself for having left it open I saw him on the floor. Yes, he does kind of look like me. I don't know why his shirt is half off like that."

Why was the corpse's shirt open, to check the tattoo?

John's tattoo was a courting gesture to his ex-wife, Cassilda, who had had a dream about a black rose. The cops wouldn't ask him about his tattoos, would they? Better put on a long-sleeved shirt to cover up the Electric Luddites on his left arm before he called them. He should check the dead man for a wallet. Find out the name of this man he didn't want to know.

The body was difficult to handle; when he lifted the buttocks to see if there was a wallet in the hip pocket, more blood and stuff came from that awful hole in the head. The guy had a wallet. It had a few bucks in it, no credit cards, driver's license, or anything that pointed to a name. It was difficult to lift the body a second time to shove the wallet back in the pocket. Would they know that he had messed with the body? Would bloodstains show this?

Had the neighbors seen or heard anything? Maybe the police were on their way now, so he had better call. Or just jump in his car and head for the border.

He had never cared for Mexican food. It had been one of the little things that led to his breakup with Cassilda.

He walked into his office. A half-finished text for *Sethos 2* was on the screen.

```
"If Sethos should use his arrows
 against the dragon, click here; if
 Sethos should run away, click
 here; if Sethos should use his
 magic flute, click here; if Sethos
 should attempt to talk to the
 dragon"
```

John picked up the phone and dialed 911.

"Hello, I want to report, I eh want to report, I eh want to report a dead man. There's a dead man in my living room. A killed dead man."

This babbling went on, with various prompts from the operator, till John was able to give him his address and the idea that the dead man was a murdered man. The operator told him several times not to leave home, and John realized that he had for the first time in his life convinced a fellow human being that he was indeed crazy.

John hung up the phone, and went to sit with the dead man.

Don't leave home. Hell, he worked as a game designer for that very reason, he was a touch agoraphobic. He left home for four reasons only. (1) To visit his mom in Amarillo. (2) To buy food. (3) To go to weird art stuff in Austin and surrounding areas. You could spot him in the weirdest venues wearing clothes that he bought from JCPenney or that his mom bought and mailed to him from garage sales back home. And (4) To play games with his friends—mainly other white guys with glasses. *Don't leave home.* Now he was going to jail, because somebody dumped a body. . . .

Why was he here?

There were a thousand other questions that rose from that seed question and they got louder and louder and louder in John's head. The combined buzzing of questions seemed to become a shout. Go away! Run away! There was nothing in his life that had prepared him for this.

A police car drove up.

Another police car drove up, this one parking in front of his driveway, so that he couldn't go jump in his car and drive off.

He walked out on the porch to meet them. He started to put his hands up, but regained his composure and stuck his hand out.

A Hispanic policewoman stepped out of the first car, a white policeman from the second.

An ambulance was pulling up.

Neighborhood kids were stopping on their bikes to watch.

My life is over.

The white policeman asked, "Are you John Reynman? Did you call nine-one-one to report a murder?"

"It could be a suicide. I called to report a body. I found a body."

"Please be calm, Mr. Reynman."

John thought he had sounded quite calm, considering.

The policewoman said, "Would you show us the body, Mr. Reynman?"

The ambulance crew was running up on the lawn. Suddenly John felt that he looked like Anthony Perkins.

"Come," he said.

You could see the body just as you stepped in the house. It's pretty hard not to look at a body in a small room—they possess a tremendous magnetism. The two ambulance attendants rushed forward to certify the death of the body, and there were lots of noises of people talking into radios. The policewoman put her hand on John's shoulder. "Could we talk downtown? We'll need to get a statement."

"Sure, let me tidy up a bit."

"I think," said the policeman, "you look fine. I think now is the best time to talk, while details are fresh in your mind."

John found himself in the backseat of the policeman's car, and they drove downtown. He realized that he hadn't even locked up his house, or saved his computer file. He asked the policeman, whose name turned out to be Dennis L. Olsen, about this.

"There will be people watching your house for you, when we get finished here, probably long after we're finished here. Don't worry, Mr. Reynman, your house is in good shape."

John realized that he should probably be protesting about

the lack of a warrant or something or did that count when you invited the police in or was that the way vampires worked? He'd done a game version of *Dracula* not long ago.

They gave him a glass of water when they took him to the questioning room. It was small and had a cork bulletin board covered with useful posters on reporting crimes and home safety. Print addict that he was, John lost himself quickly in these. He had never realized how dangerous outlets were in the home. Kind of a miracle really that he had not been electrocuted long ago.

A man in a slightly out-of-fashion gray suit walked in. He reminded John of John's late father, mainly because of his silvery hair and ruddy complexion. John had never resolved certain issues with his father, and it seemed terribly unfair for the dead to be coming back on such an already stressful day.

"Hello, I am Detective Blick. Anthony R. Blick. I investigate homicides, and I must say this looks like a particularly interesting case. I'd like to talk with you, Mr. Reynman. Now I must inform you that you are not at this time a suspect in the killing of the man whose body you found, but it is likely that you may become a suspect because of the extremely odd circumstances of the discovery. You may wish to consult with a lawyer now; however, it is not necessary. Anything you do tell us will be part of the record if we proceed to criminal proceedings."

The man hadn't even seemed to draw a breath during the long pronouncement. At the end of it he smiled, just like a salesman. John wasn't sure what he was supposed to buy.

"I don't need a lawyer, I just found a body," said John. *Possession is nine-tenths of the law.*

"Do you know the victim?"

"No."

"Are you sure that you don't recognize him?"

"Well, he looks a little like me."

"I would say he looks a great deal like you; do you have any brothers?"

"He's not my brother. I have three brothers, Matthew, who lives in Austin but we're not very close, and my older twin brothers Paul and Saul."

"It sounds like you come from a very religious family."

That was probably bad. John had read that was how you spotted a serial killer. They were bed wetters, liked to start fires, and were very religious. John had been a bed wetter. His brother Matthew liked to start fires.

"No, we weren't religious. When each of the kids was born, Dad would open the family Bible and stick his finger on the page and the closest male name would be ours."

"Good thing you didn't wind up with Cain."

"Dad was more into the New Testament than the Old."

"The corpse had a couple of tattoos on it. One of them was very new, for a rock group called the Electric Luddites. Are you familiar with them?"

"My ex-wife was a fan of theirs. They were a little punk band out of Silver City, New Mexico. I noticed the tattoo when I examined the body."

"You examined the body? Why?"

"I was looking to see if the guy had a wallet, I mean I wanted to know who he was."

"Why?"

"Well I don't know what to do if I find a body in my house—there's not a poster for it," John said, pointing at the bright-colored bulletin board.

"A good point," said Blick. "We'll have to make one. You told the nine-one-one operator that you were a freelance writer—maybe we can make one together. So how did you find the body?"

"I overslept. I felt lousy. I had sat down to work at my computer, when I realized the house sounded wrong. I could hear the birds and crickets too well, so I knew a door or window was open. I had screwed up a couple of times in the last month and left my front door partially open when I got home from dinner and games with my friends, so I figured the door was open."

"So you went into your front room and there was a dead man."

"Yeah—kind of zany, when you think about it."

Oh great.

"Zany isn't the word I had in mind," said Detective Blick. "There's nothing zany about death." Despite the grim remark, he finished his sentence with a big smile, as if the thought of something truly zany about death had caught his attention. He was looking at John's left forearm. John's tattoo stuck out about a centimeter from his short sleeve.

"Could I see that tattoo, Mr. Reynman?"

John pulled up his sleeve. *Maybe this is all a dream. Maybe my subconscious hates me, and this is all a dream.*

"Hmm, it seems you're a fan of the Electric Luddites too."

"Well not really. I had this made when I was on acid, I mean I hardly knew the group. It was my honeymoon."

Blick nodded sagely. "I'm sure it was a bad moment in your troubled youth. Perhaps you feel that you've recently brought certain issues to a close and you'd like to talk to me about them?"

For the next three hours, John repeated the story of how he found the body. Eventually he told it to a police stenographer.

John smelled really bad at this point.

Someone brought in a report that Blick read while John repeated his story.

Blick asked to see John's chest.

He stared at the black rose for a long time, almost, John thought, in reverence, then said, "We won't be needing you for a while. I'm sure you'll call us if you think of anything you want to say. I'm sure you won't be leaving town. We have much to talk about, you and I. Much to talk about."

Blick called down to the duty desk and got a policeman just going on duty to drive John back to his home.

His small home with its brown vinyl siding, and its bayonet grass guarding its windows, was wide open. There was yellow tape proclaiming "Police Line Do Not Cross" and there was much activity inside—like a termite-eaten log suddenly turned up to the daylight. Who were all these people? In the ten years that John had lived here, he had been proud of the fact that there had never been anyone in his home save whom he had invited. It had been the whole of his world.

2 The Hero Is Able

He drew a deep breath and walked in.

"Jesus! It's the dead guy," said a black man photographing John's living room.

"Aren't you people done yet?" asked John. The first thing to do was to get them out of here, then figure out what the hell was going on.

"You're Mr. um, Mr. Reynman?" asked the policewoman. It was the Hispanic woman who had come to the house hours before.

"Yes. I am glad you remembered."

"The technical detail will be out in under an hour. Look, the media hasn't got hold of this yet. If you keep your mouth shut, they don't need to be here. I'm sure you've already talked with your attorney about handling them, but I want to tell you there's very little we can do to protect you from them."

"Thanks for the tip. I—em—need to talk with my lawyer a little bit more. I'll do that while you finish up."

John walked to his office; it had been a small bedroom for the other owners of the house. His computer and his stacks of gaming magazines dominated the room. There were other people walking around in his house. He had no doubt that he was screwing up badly, and that at the horrible trial, he would suffer the consequences. Now if this could be happening to Paul and Saul, they read Erle Stanley Gardner, they never missed a *Perry Mason* rerun. In fact they could recite the lines along with the show, an eerie phenomenon out of the mouths of identical twins. He thought about calling them up for advice, but that was tired hot thinking. He flipped on the AC, which he noticed had a musty bad smell.

He had almost taken a contract to script a *Private-Eye* CD-ROM, but decided that he knew too little about the whole business to write out the different steps he could take. His whole exposure to detective fiction was Sherlock Holmes, whom he fancied himself in junior high; a single story by Raymond Chandler; and a partially remembered quote from a Laurie Anderson record, the last vinyl he had ever purchased.

The Chandler story had a hotel dick finding a dead jazz musician on his rented bed, the trumpeter King Leopardi, wearing his trademark yellow silk pajamas. The dick takes one look at him and says, "The King in Yellow," which reminds him of a book he'd read. *So*, thought John, *now I get to live it instead of reading about it.* That had always been his ex-wife Cassilda's objection to him, that he lived in a world of books by choice.

The Laurie Anderson quote was something like, "At the beginning of a detective story the hero has already died." Not too wrong—we're going to be doing everything for the next few months for *him*, that damn dead man who now owns my life.

John picked up the yellow pages and began looking for a lawyer. This was as bad as trying to think what to tell the police.

He was on his fourth call—seemed like homicide had some

sort of stigma attached to it—when the policewoman stuck her head into his office and said, "We're done. Now don't let this worry you too much. The world is full of bodies." All in a matter-of-fact Have-a-nice-day tone.

She's probably right. There are six billion people on this overpopulated globe. The odds are probably staggeringly great that one will die in your living room. John had no doubt simply been lucky that this hadn't happened before.

He locked up the house, turned on his answering machine, and took a long cold shower. John always took cold showers when he needed clarity. When he was in deadline crunch mode, showers were frequent. Showers were better than coffee.

As he lathered up his bronze hair, someone began ringing his doorbell. A neighbor? A reporter? The police? A kid selling candy? He turned off the shower and tried to be as quiet as possible. He tried not to breathe; as though the mysterious caller were equipped with some sort of superhuman hearing.

He/She/It/They rang once more. Then he could hear a truck leaving. When John realized that had to have been the UPS truck, he laughed a normal laugh for the first time in eight hours. It was about 5:00, which was when UPS made its run through his neighborhood.

He put on his shorts and a shirt his mom had mailed him from one of her garage saling expeditions and went to the door. The living room still smelled, and there was still blood on the floor. He guessed he could clean up now. There was no law that said blood had to remain on the floor, calling out for vengeance. Vengeance? Now that's a peculiar idea. He peered very carefully out the front door's spy hole.

No one in sight, but a cardboard box from Hyades Games lay on the porch.

He opened the door quickly, and grabbed the box. The guy across the street was watching him through his dirty gauze curtains. John wanted to flip him off, but instead waved ingratiatingly. The wave wasn't returned. John had the completely irrational thought that he should kill the guy because he was a witness.

John took the box inside, leaping it over the bloodstain, got a knife from his small messy kitchen, and opened the box.

There were ten copies of his latest game, *The Return of Hastur*, which was CD-ROM-based; he'd done the scripts. He'd give out four or five, and send some to friends with 'zines to review, and would wind up giving the rest of them to the charity auction at ArmadilloCon, the local SF con. Getting games was a thrill, followed by an intense depression. Before the little incident of today's corpse, John had been working hard getting deadlines out of the way. He had wanted to get everything done by October 22, so he could maybe think of doing his own work for a while. It'd been hard work all year, really. John'd written an average of twenty thousand words a month since January. (For comparison, a decent-sized novel is around one hundred thousand words.) If he stayed on this treadmill through all of the year, then by Christmas he would have completed his second million words as a game writer. No, he wasn't proud; a statistic like that is chilling, not pleasant. There were guys in the gaming business who produced three times as much as he did. John had published approximately as much as Charles Dickens had by John's age, but everybody remembers Dickens's works and not even John remembered most of his, but oh well. It beat working.

Mainly John stayed home after his divorce. His life was a kind of rust or solitude (as he knew Cassilda would phrase it).

Usually he would call his fellow game designers when he had copies of his new game. They would party. In fact last night had been just such a party for the release of Allan's new game, which was about a treasure hunt on Mars, not the real Mars, of course, a fantasy Mars where everybody wore jeweled harnesses and carried big swords. Like most of the games their little circle did, it was full of inside jokes. One of the minor villains was named Reign Mun, a phonetic rendering of John's name. God it had been hell when the movie *Rain Man* had come out. John remembered that he had a girlfriend named Rosemary that said she had similar hell in high school because the movie *Rosemary's Baby* came out. She had gone to a Catholic school too. Jesus.

He would need to call them to establish an alibi, or was that a bad idea? What did he really know about those guys? Allan claimed descent from Billy the Kid and the pirate Anne Bonney. Mark had done some time for working in a porno theater, which wasn't licensed for the area, and Bill, well he cheated during the *Acquire* game. Aaron took those mysterious long walks (like Matthew did for diabetes), and that new guy, Norman whatzisname, seemed to be hanging around to steal ideas. This wasn't good at all. He was beginning to think of his friends as suspects, but if you can't suspect your friends, whom can you suspect?

He had killed all of them fictively as well. They were minor bogeys in some of his games, and he wrote a short story every year for Christmas—perhaps this was his most Dickensian trait. Would it be a bad idea to involve them? He remembered suddenly that Blick hadn't asked for the phone number of any of the guys. Wouldn't that be normal procedure? Or did that come later? The only trial images that came to mind were from the O. J. trial, and he hadn't really watched that. The only interesting moment for him was writing a game proposal for CD-ROM to simulate the O. J. trial, just to be called *The Trial*. He gave that up in midproposal because his love for Kafka kept creeping in, and he wanted to make the whole thing revolve around Kato Kaelin. You know: K.

Maybe one of them knew a good lawyer. Bill had had a good lawyer to handle his divorce, but homicide and divorce were separate categories in all but the worst of relationships.

He put the games in the cardboard box, and the box in his bedroom, and showered again and then called Clarissa, his almost girlfriend. They had occasional sex, far too occasional for John's liking, but tonight was a good night to get laid. Now there wasn't actually a guideline that said that, but there are times for Freudian imperatives to be fulfilled.

He wasn't going to get any.

Clarissa was willing, but she had a houseguest, a cousin's chiropractor—or her chiropractor's cousin, or something. So she didn't want to go back to her place.

If I had only cleaned the blood off the floor I could've got laid.

John had decided not to tell her. They didn't have the sort of relationship that included corpses on the living-room floor. Their relationship rested more in Clarissa's willingness to be fingered on the first date, mixed with their extreme lack of social skills. After their first date, which was to see a Jackie Chan film festival at Hogg auditorium, Clarissa stopped wearing panties, and started wearing short skirts. It made the gestures of courtship much easier. John was currently engaged in such a gesture beneath the table of the vegetarian restaurant, and Clarissa was having a difficult time sitting still. The waitress had already noticed, since she was part of their usual premating ritual, and smiled mischievously.

John and Clarissa had met on a local BBS. There had been an open forum on fantasy fiction. Most of it had been deadly dull stuff—Tolkien bashing or praising sort of thing—but John had written that normal fantasy ("normal" in the T. S. Kuhn sense) was written for the moderately educated class suffering from ennui. It was for folks stuck doing dull, repetitive work, growing old while not getting laid half often or variously enough, watching other, less deserving people (the privileged and the crooks) scoop up your share of fun. So then the fantasy generates the exciting world where you're given a heroic purpose and an opportunity to use those very powers you have suspected that you had but have never been able to locate and use, except in destructive ways when shit-faced. *Magic* in these sorts of stories is not the epiphany of mainstream fiction, the burst of Grace, but simply an efficient cause, a force (you fill in the blank what kind). All these books have maps showing continents that assume a more or less quadrilateral shape because they have to fit across a badly printed double page at the front of the book: the point being that they represent a contained fantasy. There is nowhere else to go once the story is over, except on into the further volumes of formulaic repetition. John had always assumed that Clarissa had been attracted to him because of the brilliance of that post; in reality it was because of an affair she had had with her high school geometry teacher, D. B. Bowen, that caused a substantial dampening of her vagina whenever she read the word "quadrilateral." It was by this unsuspected magic that John had cast his spell over her.

As she writhed in her seat, John looked at her pale red frizzed hair, which was a dye job, her enhanced breasts, her purple eyes (thanks to the miracle of contacts), and wondered for a moment exactly what and who he was fingering. Or as he preferred to say, "scrubbing the cake pan," which had been Cassilda's preferred euphemism for female masturbation.

The peach cobbler topped with Bluebell Mexican vanilla ice cream and Clarissa's climax arrived at the same time, the soft sound of one being socially accepted for the appreciation of the other.

He had merely told her that his place was too messy. She didn't believe him, of that he was sure; after all, they had made love on his bed while it was covered in copies of gaming 'zines. But she said nothing—their relationship didn't have room for important issues.

She offered to give him a hand job in his car. They could go park somewhere, be like teenagers. He drove to a couple of spots, but didn't feel like there was enough darkness or solitude to cover the act. She pouted. He drove her back to the restaurant, where she had left her car.

He got home at 9:00, exactly twelve hours after he discovered the body. The phone was ringing, the answering machine blinking. He decided to risk the phone. It was his mother.

Things were fine on his end, nope no news at all, yes the city was way behind in its rainfall, his lantana—that's the one with the yellow and red flowers, Mom—had died. He was getting his deadlines on time, he was getting paid on time, well almost on time, hadn't talked with Matthew in awhile, yes he still saw his friend that she met that time, yes he did have a girl, no she hadn't told him the joke about life on Mars.

On her end, things were good for her, but all of her friends were sick, she was still walking in the mall every day, the cafeteria was giving out free coffee to the walkers, you really get to know those people, you know when one of them is sick they send a card to the hospital, her biggest fear now that all of her boys were away was that she would be found dead, just lying there dead in her house and all her boys would feel bad because they didn't know about it for days, oh I've already told you the story of how my great-aunt was found dead, saw your ex-wife yesterday, she's always nice to me, asked about you, said she had been thinking about you a lot, there were five lines of evidence for life on Mars, the limestone matrix, the mineralogy, the magnetite and gregite, the presence of PHCs, the apparent microfossils, and the fossilized letter from Ed McMahon telling them they might have already won, she'd call back soon.

Mom had more than an average interest in geology. She loved to take him to Palo Duro Canyon and point out the layers of the so-called Spanish Skirts, how each layer or rock held up and was changed by the layer of rock above it. The McMahon joke was high humor for Mom, and one that she couldn't share with her crowd of elderly mall walkers.

There were two messages on the machine.

"This is Detective Blick, I want to discuss some aspects of the coroner's report with you. I would like to see you as soon as convenient for you." This was followed by phone numbers, and hours, and beeper info.

"John, you old rascal, what a kick in the butt, it was great running into you at Lost Weekend. Looking forward to seeing you soon."

It was a man's voice. John thought it was vaguely familiar. He had never been to the Lost Weekend bar in his life. But somebody had, someone that could give out his unlisted phone number. Somebody that looked like him.

John played the tape about twenty times trying to identify the voice. Maybe that was a trick too.

He was tired and beat, but decided to scrub the blood off the parquet floor. He loved the floor, and he wanted to be as gentle as he could with it, but the more he scrubbed the more he realized that there would be a permanent negative marking left on it—lighter spots unpolished—that was going to really bug him. He got the box out of his bedroom again and hid the absences his cleaning had caused.

It was 2:00 in the damn morning when he was done. On a regular day, he would've gone to bed about 10:00 and got up again about 1:00 to type.

As he lay in his bed, he began playing with time. He had left Allan's at 3:00 after a game of *Acquire* and *Junta*. He had got gas at the convenience store, oh about 3:15, so he must have pulled into his house about 3:30. So the body could have been dropped anytime from 3:30 to 9:00 A.M.: since there wasn't much blood, maybe he was dead when he arrived.

3 The Magic Circle and the Triangle of Art

John Reynman woke with a hard-on because he had been dreaming of the dead shark.

Although he and Cassilda had the same hometown of Amarillo, Texas, they had met in Buenos Aires. Cassilda had had a trip there from school to study theater arts, and had decided to stay another season. He was there because his college roommate had talked him into coming with images of the beaches and sun and swimming. He had just graduated from Texas Tech, and was going to spend a year seeing the world.

They each wound up working for his roommate's uncle Eduardo. Eduardo paid nothing. They worked in a café on the beach called Fisherman's Luck. The sea was beautiful, the beaches pristine, the government totalitarian, and the hours endless. The café had no roof, so when it rained, everyone just left without paying. The staff peeled off their clothes and ran straight into the water. They always wore bathing suits underneath, and always prayed for rain because it was the only time they could swim. They always swam through the worst storms, great jagged lightning slashing at an angry sea.

They slept in the "cabins"—the little tents that the beachgoers would rent from Eduardo during the day. One morning about three, Eduardo yelled at them to wake up.

"You have to bury a shark!" he was yelling.

A huge rotting carcass of a great white had washed up on the beach. A fisherman had caught it and pulled its jaws out of its body; the teeth and jaws of a shark are valuable—especially since *Jaws* had become a big movie on Argentine television. The fisherman had tossed the jawless shark overboard, and it had washed to shore.

It stank like nothing has ever stunk. Everyone was puking. Cassilda, who had only been working there for a couple of days, gave him a bandanna and sprinkled her perfume on it. Eduardo kept yelling and lighting torches. He wanted the carcass buried. If the tourists in the morning saw the shark, they wouldn't be renting the little tents—and the smell wasn't going to pack the restaurant.

There weren't enough shovels, so some of the waiters were digging with their hands. It took hours. They were rolling the shark over into the hole just as dawn lit up the sky.

In an hour they had covered it. They staggered off to their tents. John returned the bandanna to Cassilda.

They decided to swim and get some of the stench off their bodies.

On the way to the sea, they began talking about *Jaws*, which they had both seen in the same theater. Two years and different high schools and they might as well have been on different planets.

They were sick of Argentina, mainly because they knew about people disappearing in the night, they knew about the

Argentine police. When you rode the bus downtown, and the light was just right, you could read the ghosts of the graffiti that had been sandblasted off the buildings. These palimpsests of protest on the labyrinthine walls of downtown B.A. were scarier than seeing the people actually carted off.

One day a taxi driver had told John, "I saw them burying the bodies." The guy was risking everything.

They were broke and tired and wanted to leave, and this chance encounter with someone whose memories symbolized home at its best was more relieving than the surf.

They went off a little ways.

They made love.

They still stank like dead fish, but they made sticky, sandy, smelly love. They were fucking the idea of home, of each other, of the ocean.

The tide came in around them, and a passing American tourist spotted them, and wrote, "Yesterday we saw mermaids," the first line in her limited-edition book of poetry *The Boot and the Circular Ruins*, which was mainly about the Perón regime, which kept it safely from the best-seller list.

It was the best fuck.

Ever of all time, anywhere.

In his dream there had been two women, Cassilda and another one watching.

John had begun to jack off when the phone rang.

Prudence winning over passion, he picked up the phone.

It was Blick telling him to come down as soon as he could. The autopsy results were in, and there was something about the report that John needed to know.

Hung up the phone, jacked off anyway.

He had a long shower, a good shave, a couple of Pop-Tarts, dressed slowly. He would be in control when he spoke with

Blick today. As soon as that was over, he'd get a lawyer, and then he would check out the Lost Weekend. No more screwing up.

"Best dye job I ever saw," said Blick.

"What was the victim's natural hair color?" asked John.

"We were hoping that you could tell us."

"I don't know the guy."

"You know, Mr. Reynman, I'm beginning to believe you. Unless you're a complete nut, which some of my colleagues are beginning to think. Sergeant Sanchez thinks you're a member of a bizarre cult that thinks it can escape death—by providing death a perfect facsimile. Others think that those games you write have rotted your mind. In my generation a book-burning nut named Frederic Wertham got a lot of people to believe that comic books were the source of all evil. My parents burned mine, the same thing happened to my minister. Then it was rock music. Then role-playing games, now CD-ROM games. I'm sure there was someone who protested cave paintings. These goofy hypotheses don't interest me, except that I have nothing to go on. We're getting prints, but somebody had played with the hands."

"Played with?"

"Played with is enough. We don't owe you any information, Mr. Reynman. Any information we give is a mild form of attack to break you down. You know something. I know you know something. Now it's either something you're hiding because you're guilty as sin, or it's something you've just forgotten because you're as pure as the driven snow."

"I don't think anyone is as pure as the driven snow."

"Well then you must have forgotten something."

Blick said this as though it were entirely reasonable, which

John took as a sign to end the interview as quickly as possible. There was advice against leaving town and that they would be in touch. John thought of his games where the programmer would keep people trapped until they happened to click on the right object; it was the least fun part of the game and the best metaphor for life that he knew. Christ, if this kept up there was no way he could finish his deadlines.

More phone calls and finally a lawyer would see him. He went to her office.

Her skin was flecked like buttermilk, her hair a lovely hennaed red, her lipstick a little bigger than her lips, and her manner harried. John was pleased that he still had a libido despite the stress of the day, and despairing that he would have no money at all if he got her as his attorney. He felt he was filling up the dead man's wallet.

Her name was Michelle Galen. She worked for Dewey, Bricklayer, and Crow. The name Dewey didn't make John happy; when she explained the fee schedule to him, all he could think of was "Dewwy, Cheatem, and Howe." Which Marx Brothers movie was that?

The conversation had somehow gone from his case, which was far too odd to say anything about—no doubt Ms. Galen was wondering how a certain type of client was always sent to her office—to her career woes.

"I was here when the firm was founded, five years ago. But I'm still not a partner. Why? Because my name isn't Arthur. The three partners are named Arthur, the new guy is named Arthur. They're looking at him for partnership. Are they looking at me? No. Do you think I should change my name to Arthur?"

John said, "I think Michelle is a lovely name. I had a girlfriend named Michelle in college." Where this lie came from was beyond John. John always lied like that when he was nervous. The police would crucify him.

"Do you read Perry Mason?" she asked.

"No, I don't. But you needn't worry about me, I'm not expecting Perry Mason–type miracles here."

She said, "No, no. Not that. I meant that Erle Stanley Gardner's cabin is here in Austin. It's inside the Tower building at UT on the second floor. If you're not doing anything, I could take you by it. I think it's a lot of fun. I need to drop off some things for my daughter, who works at UT. Then we could do dinner. I'm afraid I haven't been listening to your case as well as I should have. I think Arthur is a terrible name. I should start my own practice."

Standing in front of the cabin of Erle Stanley Gardner, inside a building famed for a killer's sniping spree thirty years before, while his lawyer (estranged from her Arthur-dominated firm) was dropping off a dress she had borrowed from her daughter, John Reynman was wondering if starting an affair with his lawyer would mean any professional discounts. The consultation, which he guessed was still going on, had only cost twenty dollars, and had told him what he already knew: that he was some kind of idiot talking to the police by himself. There was a little sign in front of the cabin: "It's a damn good story. If you have any comments, write them on the back of a check."—Erle Stanley Gardner (1889–1970), writing to an editor.

He was ten when Erle Stanley Gardner died; now he was thirty-eight. He wondered what ESG would have done if he had found a body on the cabin floor. Great title. *Body on the Cabin Floor.* What did ESG look like? Like TV's Perry Mason, Raymond Burr? Raymond Burr as Steve Martin in *Godzilla King of the Monsters*?

He jumped when Michelle Galen walked up behind him saying, "Did you know that—" and he jumped.

"Sorry," she said.

"Sorry," he said. "I was thinking of Godzilla."

"So was I," she said. "I'm going to change my name to that. Arthur Godzilla. I think it would inspire fear in other lawyers."

"It's not a bad choice," John allowed, "but you might go something a little softer, like Arthur Mothra."

She smiled, and her brown eyes twinkled and she said, "I was going to ask if you knew that Gardner's publishers would do anything for him? Hot and cold running secretaries, food brought to his cabin, anything. Robert Heinlein visited him once—you're an SF person right? Heinlein visited him once, decided that that was the life, created Jubal after him for *Stranger*; that's the life having everything, isn't it?"

"No," answered John—this was an old button for him—"no, because you wouldn't have your freedom. Oh the women and gold are nice enough I should reckon, but what could he do? He had to sit there pounding the keys afraid to stop. You could wind up like Michael Jackson."

"White?"

"No, unable to go anywhere, do anything. Or John Lennon or Lonnie Peters."

"I think I could take the risk of fame. Besides, if you were famous, you could pay my fee."

"If I was that famous, I would have somebody to call to dispose of the bodies. I bet celebrities do that all the time."

"Yeah, it's a service in Beverly Hills; if they don't collect the body in thirty minutes, it's free. O. J. wasn't out a dime. You, on the other hand, well I always tell my clients that you shouldn't plan on finding bodies until you're well-heeled."

"Another life screwup." John sighed. He had thought of

asking her what if the client was well hung, but it was too early for language slippage and flirting.

"Screwups are the source of life's freedom, like the lack of fame. Have you decided where to eat?"

"Have you ever been to the Lost Weekend?"

"My first marriage was the Lost Weekend."

"You married Ray Milland?"

"More or less. But no, I've seen the pub, but never stopped in. I hear they've got a great Welsh rarebit."

The pub was near campus on Lamar Street. Lamar was named after the second president of the Republic of Texas. He was a romantic dreamer, a writer of poetry. Mirabeau B. Lamar. The B was for Bonaparte—he was named after Napoleon and Count Mirabeau. He moved the capital of Texas from Houston to Austin because once while hunting buffalo on Waller Creek, he had a vision of a great white buffalo. In those days Austin was called Waterloo; there's still a Waterloo Park in Austin.

Anyone can logically see why you would want to move a capital from an established port city in safe territory to an Indian-threatened unsettled region full of bats and bluebonnets. Lamar had intended Austin to be the seat of a great empire stretching all the way through the western darkness to California, up to Oregon and down to the Yucatán. As John Reynman was fond of saying, "If you understand that Lamar is the north-south spine of Austin, you begin to understand Austin."

Michelle drove too fast for him to tell her the whole story. She must be a good lawyer, she drove a black Mercedes-Benz.

It was a little after five, U-Turn Laverne was on the radio giving the traffic report, and the pub was filling up with workers from downtown—mainly single men and women who stopped off here for a touch of after-work camaraderie as a charm against the night's loneliness and vampire light of TV. John had expected the place to reflect the film of the same name, and was disappointed that it had an ersatz English atmosphere. He didn't know if he had done the right thing bringing her here. He had told no one about the call, because it could all be coincidence, and besides, it was a new answering machine and he had screwed up and erased the evidence. If it was evidence of anything other than the fact his life had jumped its tracks.

They found a table to themselves, and talked Austin for a while, and then how odd his case was, and then she asked the obvious follow-up question to his earlier one.

"So," she said, "you been here before?"

"Eh. No."

"Then why did you pick it?"

"Why did you marry Ray Milland?"

"Marrying drunks is easy—didn't you say you were one of the great divorced?"

"Yeah, but not because of drinks, because I was a screwup. I was a dead guy after I got married. I didn't like going out, I didn't like taking risks, I didn't seek after the mysteries. I just went to sleep. Cassilda was always trying out new things. Once she suggested we share a woman in bed, which would have been most guys' dream, but I was worried that she might like it too much. I didn't even go to museums anymore. I don't know. She left, and I woke up way too damn late."

"You're right. You were a screwup."

She had Welsh rarebit; he had nachos with far too many jalapeños.

The wait staff changed shift. *Jeopardy* came on and everyone watched the TV and asked it questions.

The new waiter came by and looked at John and said, "Let me remember, Shiner bock, right?"

So John said, "Right."

Michelle ordered the same.

"I thought," she said, "that you never came in here."

"He's probably seen me elsewhere. You know waiters, they circle from bar to bar, restaurant to restaurant."

"Or," she said, "you've got one of the faces that just looks familiar, like any dead guy on the living-room floor. You knew to come here. Why?"

"It's just luck."

"Don't hide things from your attorney. That is distinctly bad luck. You *knew*."

"OK. I—"

The waiter was back with the beers.

Michelle asked the waiter, "I don't think you waited on us last time we were here, did you?"

The guy paused and said, "I don't think I've met you ma'am, but I met Taylor at one of the Magic Circle lectures. I'm sorry—is it Taylor or Thomas?"

John hesitated and said, "Thomas, but you can call me Tom." He stuck his hand out like an idiot, hoping he'd guessed right, or he would have put another stratum of illusion between him and the bedrock of truth. What would Mom say? Oh Christ—John-Thomas. *I really am a dick*, he thought.

The waiter shook his hand with evident dismay, apparently having reached the same conclusion through a different line of reasoning.

"I hope we see you next Saturday," he said, his tone saying something else.

"Sure you will," said John. "Um, I forget—what is next Saturday?"

"Dr. Niles will be talking about the Command to Look."

The waiter walked away.

"Well, Tom, I think we'll have a great deal to look at then, don't you?"

Alex Trebek agreed on the TV; that was the *Jeopardy* question.

4 Smelt Was Comfort Food

They didn't sleep together the first night, nor the second, but the revelation of the name gave them enough joy the third night.

Cunnilingus was always for John the great stress reliever. This had helped his dating in the eighties immensely, but its practice went beyond the great popularity it brought him. It allowed him to bury his troubles and anxieties into another— or to place his ecstasy in a place where he could call upon it. To plunge into a warm wet comfort that tasted of the primordial seas. It was beyond mere sex; it was a moment when evolution could begin anew. He had often had the fantasy of the perfect office, where when things were too stressful or too joyful he could go down on his (perfectly airbrushed attractive) cubemate. The lack of such jobs had driven him from the workplace into freelance work, which at least offered other reliefs.

He ate Michelle with great and unending gusto, and after her sixth orgasm, she had a type of vision. She was not wholly unprepared for this; similar circumstances during an Eagles concert a few years before had likewise lifted her eyes to the noetic realms.

She saw herself in an airy ancient hall lit by the breathing light of candles. John was with her looking for his keys, insisting that they needed them to open a small wooden box that sat between two candles. She kept trying to get John to relax, telling him that the box was already open, that it had been open for years, but that no one had noticed.

John didn't find his keys, but pulled a simple carved stone from his pocket.

She tried to explain to John that the stone was what had been in the box.

Her seventh orgasm came and obliterated the vision.

She spent the night and didn't tell him the vision till the morning, which was Saturday.

The name the police had discovered was Taylor Keziah Mason. They were considering a case against John. Michelle Galen warned Blick against harassing her client, citing several ominous-sounding rulings. "Don't worry, they don't know anything, yet."

Michelle had learned the name from the police on Thursday. The effect of the name opened some huge energy in John. He had done precious little since discovering the body, but somehow just knowing that the body had a name was a relief. It wasn't some strange supernatural force in his life. That person had a history, a real history, and that was a saving grace. He could be studied and viewed as a separate entity, not merely as some reflection of his being.

When John felt happy, other than his desire to share it with a mature female member of the species, he also took care of billing. The gaming industry is notoriously slow in paying the folks that it owes. Days, weeks, months go by. John's recent lift from Role Playing Games (RPGs) to writing the scripts for CD-ROMs and text-based games had brought more zeros to his paycheck, but no faster flow of the aforementioned zeros.

When he wasn't on the phone to a particularly irritating publisher in Chicago, he was typing away at *Sethos 2*, a game based on a German novel that had been the prototype for Mozart's *The Magic Flute*. Sethos's life had come to resemble John's own, as is always the case when you have to write quickly. John wondered how many troubled relationships had become orc battles, how many frigid wives had become lich queens, how many birthday parties had become royal feasts. There had been a brief period when it had been fashionable among Austin game designers to work the names of every little shop on a certain block of Burnet Road, not far from John's house, into as many games as they could. Not in any big way, of course, and not in any way that might raise the ire of the shopkeepers, or the greed of their lawyers. Just a passing note, something the character sees on the way to more important action. This hidden form of signature also proved who really wrote the product. Some companies preferred vast products to exist under only one name because they felt that the public wouldn't like seeing too many names on the box. John had never followed that logic, but in order to survive as a freelancer you learn never to pay too much attention to your customers' logic, just their specifications. One of John's trademarks had been Ron and Don's Chat and Chew, which he had managed to work into some pseudomedieval games as a biscuit and roll cart. He had never met Ron nor Don nor bought anything to chew whilst chatting; the kolache shop had been a theater that Cassilda used to enjoy going to. Too many experimental plays there, too much new stuff, so it had gone belly-up.

He had just finished a scene about Sethos, having come to the conclusion that the location of the Magic Flute was in Goldenflower. He sought the aid of Sophis, who was buying biscuits at Ron and Don's Chat and Chew. No one else played the place game anymore, because the old gaming gang had stopped writing except for Allan, Mark, and Bill. But he continued to do so, because he had some need to mythologize the place he lived. It was Friday afternoon, and Michelle called up that Mason had been a resident of Danvers, Massachusetts. He had taught math at a community college, and he had been missing for three years.

That was enough details to push John into ecstasy. This was a real guy, bounded by time and space. A small problem that could be studied. He was so excited that he expressed his desire to eat Michelle.

Although she thought the connection between math instruction and sex was a bit vague, she also hadn't had a partner in two years. So things proceeded at a fevered pace.

Years later, after the Change, she often expressed surprise that she hadn't gotten a speeding ticket on the way to John's house.

Long after the sex and at the beginning of the where-do-you-want-to-go-to-eat, she told him about her vision. She thought it would be a great bonding moment for him because she was a great believer in the unconscious. She often received courtroom strategies in her dreams. The purse strategy had been one of her best. She would arrive in court looking really flustered and drop her purse, scramble to pick it up, and generally act like a ditz. This had two advantages: it convinced the witnesses that she was too scattered to be much of a threat, and it would show off her legs and behind to the jury. Her first questions were a little vague, as though she didn't really know what the case was about, a little flattering to the witness if he or she was an "expert" witness. And then she would go in for the kill, having spent five or ten hours learning the controversies in the witness's specialty. She had the purse dream the day she found out that her father had Alzheimer's.

John hated the dream.

It was too much like what he did for a living. If he could only point and click on the right image—was it the carved stone? Was it the box? The thing that John feared most was that his life would come to resemble his games, the way that his games came to resemble his life. This cosmic cannibalism would be his doom. He had many unhappy fantasies of sitting at his keyboard and it just eating him, each key rising up like a shark's tooth and breaking his skin. Now his life was taking on such absurd dimensions.

"Eating," said Michelle, "as you well know, needn't be a frightening experience; it is based on trust. I think I want a hot dog."

Michelle's fellatio was the best he had ever had, even better than Cassilda's, which was Olympic class. For her it was the great moment of giving. To John's astonishment she came while sucking him off. Look, Ma, no hands.

It occurred to them later in the day, while they were eating omelettes at Humpty's and Michelle was telling about the purse strategy, that the single person's friend Mr. Latex hadn't been around. John had been too concerned with saving his life to worry about saving his life, and Michelle (although she didn't say so) wanted John not to be angry with her for telling about the vision. They looked at their omelettes—John had a ham and cheese, Michelle spinach—and resolved to be more careful in the future. The conversation drifted on to Michelle's father. She said that the day she had to put him in a nursing home was the toughest day of her life, even harder than burying her mother.

"He was one of those old men who as he got older began to speak of death as though it was an ever-receding event. Further away when he was seventy than when he was sixty. It was as though he waited too long and became unfit for death."

She saw him once a month. It ate her up with guilt to see him so seldom, but it killed her when he had no idea who she was, imagining her a nurse, or a fellow inmate. John challenged that noun, but no she said, that place is a prison without bars, and I have devoted my life to keeping people out of prison.

"Because they're innocent?"

"Who knows innocent? My job is to take men out of hell."

Tomorrow, Saturday, was the day she visited her father, but she said she wasn't going to go because it would upset her too much to go to the Lost Weekend and hear Dr. Niles's lecture.

"No, we'll go together to see your dad in the morning and we'll go to the lecture that night."

"Well, gee, what will we do in the afternoon?"

"Stopping by a drugstore seems to be a first step to that."

They drove to Eden-mart, a supermarket, instead. It had a huge post oak tree growing in an atrium in the middle of the store. One of those only-in-Austin sort of places. Its logo was a giant apple, which given the name would suggest that the fruit of knowledge of good and evil might be purchased there. No doubt the *Weekly World News* was referred to. John apologized for going postal about her vision; he was in his heart flattered that his cunnilingus could make people see things.

Michelle misread the apology as some sort of approval and told him that the only way to make life worth living was to seek after the mysteries.

John got silent again. Cassilda used to say the same thing, the exact same thing, and his lethargic approach to it had ended their marriage.

The outside of the rest home was beautiful.

The inside smelled.

Why does the slow death of old age have to have such a smell? More than the urine and the loose bowel, more than the disinfectants, there was a smell in the old who waited expectantly for death. It was all too much like a ghost story found in one of those novels with a chintzy black cover. The young hero smells the smell of the invisible monster. "By their smell you shall know them," he reads in some forbidden text of eldritch lore. Once or twice he captures a whiff of the dread smell. It spoils his wedding feast, it frightens him after he has slain a dragon. An invisible monster is always worse than a dragon. Then one day he begins to smell it all the time. At first it is faint, as though the monster were far away, perhaps toying with him. Then it is closer; perhaps it has come to live in the walls of the haunted manor. But then one day, the hero discovers that it is his *own* body. The monster has taken his body away from him, and there is nothing left to fight the monster with.

Michelle's father had had a "bad" night. He was in restraints, in something the nurses called a "gerry-chair."

"They didn't bring me my breakfast," were his first words. His breakfast was on a tray in front of him.

"Here it is, Dad, here."

The next few minutes were the old man getting angry and Michelle trying to get him to see what was in front of him. She even tried to feed him like an infant, and like an infant he spat out his food.

John had to leave the room a moment then. He had an awfully strong gag reflex. She cleaned her father up, John came back in, and she tried to introduce John to him.

It was as though he were so old, he had no room for anything new. She wanted him to see John, to notice him.

But John wasn't there for the old man, as though he were a void, a patch of air that held no more interest than any other. Indeed considerably less, since no glowing dust motes streamed through him.

John acted like the old man saw him, shook his hand, joked that he had a beautiful daughter.

"They didn't bring me my breakfast," were his last words as they left.

John just held her for a long time in the parking lot. Words were a bit out of place here.

That afternoon she showed John an interesting trick.

She cleaned off her vagina with a wipe.

"It has to be dry for this to work."

She unrolled a large-sized lubricated condom a third of the way, and inserted the tip in her vagina. She coaxed the head of his penis into the condom and told him to thrust slowly, unrolling the rest of it on his shaft as he entered, and keeping her vaginal muscles as tight as she could. When the condom was on, she completely relaxed her vagina, which sucked at the hard member admirably.

"Who says safe sex can't be fun?"

"Did you learn this at law school?"

"Self-paced study."

The twilight sky glowed with lemon and salmon and burnt orange clouds. It was a beautiful Texan sky, one that inspired the common Austin bumper sticker that asked, If God is not a graduate of UT, why is the sky burnt orange?

John got Michelle to drive. He didn't like driving. It was the one part of his masculinity he doubted. He could be propositioned in public rest rooms, stand up to a gang of teenagers, ask for a raise when he thought he deserved one (back in the days when he was a wage slave), but cars defeated him. He never felt confident driving at seventy miles an hour, never knew what the hell to say to a garage mechanic, who he assumed was cheating him from the get-go, never chatted with his friends about them, couldn't identify most brands. He had been known to grow faint just inhaling the fumes of a muffler repair shop. In this, John knew, he wasn't a man. When it was at its worst, John would believe that he would die in a car wreck; when it was at its best he merely assumed that garage mechanics always laughed at him when he left their garage.

Michelle pulled into the Lost Weekend parking lot, parking next to a papyrus white Mercedes-Benz 220 SE.

John stepped out to look more closely at the car.

He would have heard another car squealing away, but he was momentarily deafened by the bullet whizzing past his ear, and striking the Mercedes roof.

5 The Command to Look

John dropped to the pavement the moment he realized that he had been shot at. Like any suburban white male, he had been shot at hundreds of times in his fantasies. He had saved stores and beautiful women. It was much louder in real life. People came running out of the Lost Weekend. A short thin man with a shaved head ran over to the Mercedes.

"Son of a bitch, that car is thirty-six years old. No one's shot it in thirty-six years."

The man was dressed all in black. He would have been a handsome fellow except his eyes were slightly too large. It's hard to guess the age of a bald man.

"My God, man, have you been shot?"

"No," John said, standing up. "Just shot at, I think."

"Son of a bitch," the man said, "I'm Dr. David Niles. Now you've been to my lectures before. Taylor—er—em—Mason, isn't it? You were at my 'Cup of Grue' lecture. Oh hell, what am I thinking, we need to call the cops. Come inside. The rest of you don't stand around on the street if there's somebody driving around shooting at the pub."

The change in the little man's voice was impressive, and everyone did as he said.

Just inside the pub, Dr. Niles called out, "Mr. Bildad, would you be so kind as to summon the constabulary? It appears that some ruffian has mistaken one of your clients for a type of target and shot Betsy instead."

Michelle trailed along, unhappy that suddenly this weird guy seemed to be in charge.

Dr. Niles sat John down at the bar. "If you would, Mr. Bildad, give this man a beer and put it on my tab. I will wish to speak to the police about my car."

Suddenly John realized that he did not want to talk to the police if he was to be identified as Mr. Mason.

"I'm sure they weren't shooting at me," he said. "It was some random thing. I mean why would anyone shoot at me?"

"Well I doubt that they were shooting at my car. Older Mercedes are very popular, you know, scarcely anyone shoots at them." Dr. Niles patted John's shoulder, and leaned in close to his ear, whispering, "Do you not want us to call the police?"

John's eyes answered. Dr. Niles nodded slightly.

"Mr. Bildad, why don't you let me and Mr. Mason call from your office. I'm sure we can make a quick report, and then I'll be able to give my lecture uninterrupted."

Bildad, a stout older English gentleman, seemed to relish the conspiratorial atmosphere. It seemed to John that everyone but he and Michelle were in on this. Dr. Niles pushed him toward Bildad's office, and Michelle started to follow, but Dr. Niles said, "I think you may wish to wait outside, miss."

Michelle looked like she wanted to argue, but clearly she felt the weird atmosphere of the place as well. This had been a displaced English pub, a little corny perhaps, but now the twenty or so men and women waiting for the lecture were a little too intense. It was too much like a bad movie where they were about to warn John and her not to go out on the moors.

"I'll wait," she said, "right here."

She sat on the barstool closest to the door to Bildad's office.

The office was small and not as well air-conditioned as the rest of the bar. Even in late September, well early October, Austin was hot. It had been a hot and dry year.

John sat on the wobbly chair in front of the messy desk, where he imagined Bildad gave the worst to the careless barkeep or the clumsy waitress.

"You've always been a quiet sort, Mason, the last kind of man I'd suspect to be in any trouble," said Dr. Niles.

"Well. I'm not. Not really you see. I'm not," said John.

"Being a target is being in trouble. As I said in my last lecture, 'We're all targets at least once, when death takes us away.' I remember you nodding your head at that one. I wondered if you were on the verge of being a target. I hoped that you would wake up."

"Wake up?"

"If we don't awaken, we meet our death asleep. Don't you think it's important to meet your death knowing that you have lived, Mr. Mason?"

"I've never thought about death."

"We never think about death or life, Mr. Mason, that's why we sleep all the time."

"I feel awake right now."

Dr. Niles gave him a piercing look, a stupendous stare. He nodded. "Yes, you could be waking up, but if awakened, will you see? If you see, will you act? Or will you drift back off to sleep?"

John answered in a voice that he had never heard before, "I hope to act."

God, he was hopeless, he was talking philosophy with a bald weirdo in an ersatz pub.

"Well, Mr. Mason, if you don't want me to call the police, I shan't. Let us look of good cheer as we meet our audience."

Dr. Niles rose up and led John back into the bar. Someone had got a lectern ready. John and Michelle took seats on the third, or last, row of folding chairs. When Dr. Niles spoke he seemed to have a spotlight on him.

John's hearing began to fade shortly after he sat down. There had been a sharp deafness shortly after the bullet had whizzed past his ear, and then sound had returned, but now it was slowly leaving again as Dr. Niles began speaking on the—well he was having a little trouble following the talk—on the visual impact of the occult. Or at least of occult information. Dr. Niles kept using examples from the art of advertising, mentioning why certain logos stuck in our minds. The deafness was a kind of drowning. It made him watch the audience more carefully. Their faces, even Michelle's, were strangely rapt. Perhaps there was something more to this lecture than he realized; perhaps some quality of voice that Dr. Niles possessed had them all in some sort of trance. He tried to catch a few phrases.

Dr. Niles was talking about how he had begun his quest for wisdom. He had had an encounter with a street person who pissed on his shoes. Some vile, horrid little man with blond hair and tattoos, a human advertisement for a rock group. Instead of apologizing, the guy had hit him up for money. Dr. Niles had refused, so the guy had pulled a knife and got Dr. Niles to hand over his wallet. He had then slashed Dr. Niles on his right arm, while telling a tale about some woman who had done him wrong.

Dr. Niles had tried to put the incident behind him, but the "shock" of it had awakened him. Years ago, when he was a student, a similar shock had changed him from someone who couldn't write to someone who could in about fifteen minutes. His favorite professor had called him into his office and said, "I like you, David, but you just can't write for crap." Now he had known how not to dangle a participle, but he had just been careless, just been doing things while asleep. It took him a few rough minutes to realize that he could write if he just did it while awake. He didn't need to go buy some How-To-Write books, he just needed to wake up. But the shock of the encounter with the man in the alley really awakened him. The man in the alley was everything that Dr. Niles didn't want to be, everything he hated in himself and mankind. So he decided to seek out the woman. All great quests begin with seeking out the woman. Michelle turned and smiled at John.

Dr. Niles figured that the woman must be a sort of saint if she had earned the ire of such a piece of filth. He had her whole name, and he set out to find her. It should be a simple matter, she lived in Austin, but by the time he had screwed up his courage to speak with her—it was after all a difficult social situation, "A beggar pissed on my shoes, slashed my arm, and mentioned your name"—she had left for Morocco.

So Dr. Niles, an art instructor at the University of Texas at Austin, went after her during summer break. He found that she had lived briefly in Fez, a two-thousand-year-old city that had never been mapped, but she had left Fez for Athens to meet with her spiritual teacher.

He spent the fall looking for her teacher, drinking the resinated wine, enjoying pilaf and meats enriched with the native oil, and speaking such Greek as Heaven permitted. Finally, on the street of Hermes, in front of one of the most intact temples, the Temple of Theseus, he had the sought-for audience. The magus had an endearing smile. Yes, he was the woman's teacher, but he himself was a pupil of another, and he mentioned the other's name and location. And Niles sought and found and sought again, moving up the ladder of human goodness until he neared the Source. When Niles found the Source—

By this time John's hearing had vanished altogether. He decided that as soon as the lecture was over, he was going to get Michelle to drive him to an emergency clinic. It didn't matter if the police entered the scene now, there was clearly too much against him. Dr. Niles told a joke and everyone contorted in silent laughter.

John began to fidget. There was a copy of the *Chronicle* on the bar near him. He read the headlines, but thought it was too rude to pick up the newspaper and read the personals section. The personals were the big draw for the free paper. They provided material for fantasies and for jokes alike. The people that placed them, John decided, must be very sincere in their desire to reach out and touch someone. John had been eaten by that desire for years. Cassilda had fulfilled it for four years, but he had screwed that up. No one else, not even when the sex was great, touched on that need at all. He remembered when his father had died, his mom had talked about the need, but Cassilda was with him then, so he didn't understand. It might be a Hallmark card sentiment, but no one understands love until he has lost it.

John suddenly thought about what Dr. Niles had said about doing things when you're asleep. He had had his whole marriage while he was asleep. It wasn't some damn art form to do marriage right—millions of people do that—it was a matter of approaching it with the understanding of its importance. That's a simple thing. Water at an oasis is a simple thing.

John began to cry, quietly, and excused himself to the men's room. He found a stall, closed the door, and cried awhile.

He read the graffiti.

He cried.

If I awaken, will I see?

If I see, will I act?

He suddenly became afraid of his deafness. All his life he would have known if someone else was in the men's room with him. He would have heard the door, the splash at the urinal, the tap turned on, the sighs and moans of the constipated.

Although he hadn't done anything, he flushed and got up to leave. There was a young man in a leather jacket drying his hands in front of the mirror.

The young man spoke and John could barely make out what he said. The young man said, "I hope the urinal doesn't start following me."

"What?" John asked, apparently too loudly.

"Like Denial's story, someone pissed on his shoes and he started following them. You'd be in a bad way, if urinals started following you. Down the street you go, and here they come, clanking up behind you. You know, I think I'll paint that."

"Are you a painter?" John asked. Cassilda had fantasized about being a painter.

"People that paint things generally are."

"I thought the point of the story was that he followed the woman."

"I'm not into the point of the story, I'm here for the visuals—isn't that why he calls it the 'Command to Look'?"

"I hadn't thought about it."

"You're the guy who was shot, weren't you?"

"Shot at."

"Well why are you here if not to look?"

Most of John's hearing was back.

"I'm here to find things out."

"Find out anything?"

John's great moment was here; he could tell this guy about being awake in marriage. He did really know something for the first time in eight and thirty years, and it wasn't the right time to tell anyone. But his hearing was back. He smiled a dummy smile and went back into the bar.

The lecture was ending, people were going up to talk with Dr. Niles, and Michelle walked over to him.

"Well," she said. "I think we know less than we knew before."

"I don't know about that," John said. He walked forward and put ten dollars in the black beret on the barstool next to Dr. Niles's lectern.

Niles turned and said, "Thanks. I hope our next talk won't scare you too much."

John had a sudden turn in his bones, the feeling his grandmother used to describe as "Someone just walked over my grave." Niles wasn't talking about a lecture. The lectures weren't scary at all—unless you really thought about what it means to be doing everything while asleep. Marching off to war, to the voting booth, designing games to help the sleepers sleep more deeply.

Maybe there were games that could make people wake up. But if awakened, would they see?

"I'm taking you home," said John, and he gently grabbed Michelle's arm.

"Hey, I'm driving, but my place is fine."

They drove off in the night. Michelle lived in an apartment downtown, big and roomy, full of art and books and tall vases with peacock plumes and neat movies. The trash was full of microwave trays, and the refrigerator looked more like a bachelor's. There were pictures of her daughter, Carol, one picture that showed the ex-husband and Carol and Michelle in Juárez buying one of those sets of stuffed frogs playing in a bad band forever.

"What did you think of Dr. Niles's lecture?" asked John.

"I kinda fell asleep during it. The first part about how to construct a visual image that attracts attention, provokes an emotional response, and then stays in memory—that was fascinating, but when he started talking about Egypt and electricity and virtual reality, I sort of fell asleep, and I had this dream about all of us walking out of the bar onto a snowy plain in some postapocalyptic world. We were streaming away toward some goal, some new goal that we all understood, and there was some man on a tower behind us in a cloak of scarlet, a small dark man, with the face of someone that really knew something. I was so proud, because it was you."

"I don't follow any of this at all. I don't remember anything about Egypt—of course I spent part of the time in the men's room."

"Are you OK?"

"Yeah, just shaken up. I'm not shot at every day."

"Do you want to do anything tonight?"

"You mean sex? No."

"Why did you want to come here?"

"I just wanted to see this place, to see you, to drink you in."

She lit a couple of candles and turned off the overhead light, and walking hand in hand she took him to each picture, each book, each souvenir and began telling its story.

6 Math Books from the Dead Man (with Musical Interlude)

He woke alone.

For a moment he was afraid at being in a strange bed.

He had read an SF paperback years ago, about some hero who kept dying and being reborn in different bodies. He hadn't really trusted his own body since seeing the double.

But he was in her apartment, and that meant love and safety, didn't it?

He got up, found a note that she had gone into work because of important information, and that he should raid the fridge.

Not too tempting booty there, my maties.

He called her office but the voice mail system was goofed up and kept asking him to press 666.

He called a cab, left a note, and rode home.

His neighbor from across the street stood in the yard. He knew he needed to talk to the guy, to make friends; he knew the guy would be at the trial. John hated him, mainly the smell of liquor on him.

John waved and walked over to the neighbor. The smell

didn't hit till he was five feet away. John realized that he couldn't recall the man's name even though he had lived there for five years—moving in a couple of years after John's divorce.

"Hey," said John.

"Hey, you're a popular man," said the neighbor.

"How do you figure?"

"Police always busting up your parties. I used to give parties back when I had my shit together, you know, back when I was married."

"I hope my—um—parties haven't disturbed you."

"No, someone should have fun. That one the police broke up would have been a lot of fun. I could be popular with the police if I could figure out how you got that body in there."

"What body?"

"The one they carried away. See, if I was smarter I'd be popular. I spend all my time learning the six Korean words. Where I work, you see, is Korean and they have these six words that you're supposed to know. If they stop you in the hall like you're on your way to take a leak, they ask you and you're supposed to know them. They rhyme or something with the company's name in English. I can't learn them at all, so I spend my nights awake drinkin', watchin', and trying to learn the six words. But even though I was watching, I didn't see you bring in the other body."

"Did you talk with the police about the other body?"

"No, I tried to talk to that Chicana but I only got as far as talking about the six words and she thanked me. I think she's prejudiced against Koreans. If I could figure things out I would talk to them, though, because the police are good folk to be popular with. On my days off, like today, I could go down to that Chinese restaurant, you know the one down there that used to be an A&W, and I could talk with them. Maybe I could help with other cases."

"Well you seem pretty smart to me. What did you figure out?"

"You won't go tell the police telling them it's your idea?"

"Oh no. Credit where credit is due, my mamma always said," said John Reynman, feeling like he was quoting Forrest Gump.

"Well it's like this. I had the first three words down when you drove off to meet your friends about six-thirty. Then I watched some TV, then I took a little nap. When I got up I had a couple of beers and discovered that I only knew the first word and half the second word. So I started trying to chant the words in the dark. While I was doing my magic spell, the dog down the street, that goddamn yappy dog, you know the one, worse than a goddamn car alarm, starts yapping, so I stop my chanting and look toward the north. There you was coming down the street trying to act real nonchalant. I saw you good under the streetlight. I wondered what had happened to your car. You walked on down the street about midnight or so, up to your front door, and then you took a real long time opening the door. You was whistling 'The Yellow Rose of Texas.' Finally you got the door open, and you walked in, you flipped the lights on once, pulled the shades, and flipped the lights off. I figured you was drunk because you couldn't work your key very well. Then about two, you drove up, parked your car, and went in the side door. I saw your bedroom light for a while. Then I snoozed. I guess you had sobered up and went off to find your car. That's the responsible thing to do. I don't believe in driving while drunk. I even kept a red ribbon on the door of my car when I had a car. Then I tried to sleep some more. About four-thirty a man and lady drove up and parked in front of your house. They stayed there awhile arguing. I couldn't hear most of it. Then the man got out and walked around the house. A minute later he left through your front door—it was about five. He looked over at where I was behind the dark blinds of my house. Suddenly I found that I could say all six words in a row, and I was so happy that I jacked off and went to bed. But when I woke up I was too sick to go into work, and then I saw the two cop cars parking in front of your house. I tried to tell the police but they don't care about the six words, they don't give a damn."

"Did you get a good look at the car of the man who came in last?"

"Hey, he's your friend."

"Well, I don't know about that, but if you could meet him I bet you could say the six words."

"You got a point there. I thought I saw him clearly, but I can't bring him to mind. So how did you get the extra body in there?"

"That, I truly do not know, and if you can figure it out you will be very popular with me."

"Do you think you can teach me the six words?"

"Do you want to try now?"

"No I don't do no learning on Sunday. God didn't do no learning on Sunday, he learned about the universe the first six days."

"Well, you take care."

"You want a beer?"

"I'll pass."

The red-nosed neighbor went back in.

God bless the Koreans and their six words, thought John. If the neighbor had seen the double walking to the house at midnight, that meant he must have been in the house when John arrived. That was too scary. The double must not have wanted to kill him. He could have picked him off the first second John walked in the door, or worse yet walked up on him while he was asleep. No, that didn't make sense either. If the double had wanted to talk, he would have just met John at the door, or used the phone or the mail for Christ's sake.

Now if the double walked here, he might have parked somewhere to the north. That's a good idea.

John began walking to the north, and the neighbor's yappy dog (you know the one) began barking at him. It was warm, even for early Austin October. He went straight down his street, then one over, then one over the other way, and so on and so forth until he had walked for an hour and saw it.

The car was a similar make and model to his own. It was the same faded red color. It had Massachusetts plates. Now Mason was from Massachusetts. There were a few autumn leaves stuck to the car windshield. It might not have been driven for a few days. He looked at the house it was parked in front of. Nobody seemed home, but it was noon on Sunday, and people do sleep in. Besides, what would he ask them—Is this your car, 'cause if it's not, I think it's evidence in a case I've never been formally charged with?

On the passenger's seat was a big trade paperback, *Computers, Pattern, Chaos, and Beauty* by Kirsten Munchower. On the side of the book, written in Magic Marker across its pages to proclaim ownership, was the name MASON. There was another book beneath, but he could make out nothing about it.

The car's doors were locked.

He walked to the convenience store three blocks away. He called a cab. Cab companies usually have locksmithing.

The cab came and carried him back to the car. It took the cabbie about five minutes to open the door. John died a thousand deaths waiting to see if the curtains would part at the small green house with the white picket fence.

They did. A bored-looking black woman checked out the scene, but she didn't come running out.

John paid the twenty-five dollars and picked up the books. He opened the glove compartment and took the things out of there too. He closed up the car. He started to lock it, but realized that he might want to get something else out of it. He should have got the trunk open too. Maybe the trunk held something. You could put a body in a trunk. Didn't they always find bodies in trunks?

The second book was *The Way Out*. It too was written by an Austin writer, James M. Cassutto, published by a local press—Byatis—in 1904. It was a small, thin book bound in butter-brown leather. On the inside page was an "Ex Libris Taylor Keziah Mason." There were several passages heavily underlined.

"Hey, you."

The black woman had come out of her house.

"Yes, ma'am," answered John.

"That your car?"

"Ee uh no. It belongs to a friend of mine, who's in the hospital. He asked me to get him something to read. I couldn't find his key at his apartment."

Oh great, just dig more.

"You live around here. I've seen you taking walks in the morning."

True enough. John walked every morning.

"Yes, ma'am. I live up the street."

"Why did your friend park here?"

"He joined me on a walk one morning. You know he just drove up, saw me walking, walked with me, then got sick."

"Well I sure hope he gets better. I had been wondering about the car."

"Yes, ma'am, I'll get him to move it as soon as he's well, but he's awful sick, so it may be a while."

There were more pleasantries about the fall weather and then John walked home.

He wondered where Mason's body was. The police had surely done all they were going to do with it, and they knew who he was, so surely the body was being shipped back home. They would know what car he drove, if that little Taurus was his, and then they would find it—and it would have his fingerprints on it and that weird story that he had just told the black woman, and before long his drunken neighbor would get past the six words and would have something to say that was cogent and somehow make things worse. And he walked faster, and was more out of breath, and walked faster, holding the books very tightly, and by the time he saw his house and that Michelle's car was parked out front, he found that his chest hurt a lot. He meant to yell out to her, but he was too upset, so he broke into a stumbling run. He wanted to get to her, to tell her to stay the hell away from him, that he was so dangerously stupid that he would ruin everything and that he didn't want her hurt because he loved her. He didn't want her to be afraid at not finding him home. As he ran up and heard her ringing the doorbell, he saw that his drunken neighbor was crossing the street to talk to Michelle. He pushed a little harder, and they both turned and looked at him.

He pushed some more. Then all three met on his front yard. He opened his mouth and vomited onto the lawn.

"No sir," said the neighbor, "I don't understand why you're popular at all. That's just not the way to say hello to a lady."

He pushed the two books into Michelle's hands, sort of half fell back onto a sycamore tree, and cried.

7 The Third Attempt (with References to the History of Gaming)

Tuesday, before he was visited by the Three Men, John took a walk. Walking is the best way to develop the self, because of the eerie brilliance you have while walking. If you only had someone along with you, you could explain anything to them, give them a crystallization of your life experience so they wouldn't have to make the same dumb mistakes that you've made your whole sorry-ass life. Walking, by yourself, is the key to personal immortality because it helps so much with the crystallization of the soul.

Monday had been a good day. Michelle said that since the police hadn't brought charges by now, she figured that they didn't have anything.

He had worked on his current projects, and had even got a call from an old friend who had first got him interested in gaming. The guy had a neat world with a great world history. There was this mythical book about the great city called Freegate. It was written backward, with the latest history at the beginning and then as you progressed you went further and further into the misty past. The end of the book was codices in an unknown tongue. In the gaming world there had been an attack by all the forces of darkness—orcs, goblins, trolls, and so forth—against the great city. The attack was ominously called the First Attempt.

He was ready to do the seventh level of his Sethos game, and as with all beginnings he started off with a walk. He hadn't intended to walk past Mason's car, and when he did he didn't notice it. There was a good reason for that.

It wasn't there.

Now that is what is called a multivalued event.

He walked home and decided to read the two books he had taken from the car.

The Way Out was heavy-handed mysticism. He'd never read anything like it in his life, and found it hard going. The book's premise was that we live in a world of much greater freedom than we believe it to be, that most of our restrictions are self-imposed. Some of that idea was easy to grasp; it was the kind of insight books on optimal psychology suggested. Other ideas, like extreme longevity compressed into a single lifetime, didn't seem so rational. On the other hand, he had felt that he had lived several lifetimes in the last few days, so he could almost go along with Cassutto: "For the Adept the intensity of life is the key to Life, even to long Life. Changing perception is the Great Work." A lot of capitalization seemed to be the earmark of the writing. Perhaps Cassutto needed CAPITALS to wake up his sleeping readers.

Computers, Pattern, Chaos, and Beauty by Kirsten Munchower was much easier going. It was a treatise on the philosophical implications of fractals, those mathematical structures that needed computers to make them visible. First, mankind had had to invent imaginary numbers; then mankind had had to invent a machine that could do thousands of iterations. Then the patterns that replicated themselves in an ordered beautiful way no matter how small you looked at them emerged. How much of human life was like this? How much were the biggest patterns—say falling in love with daring women over years—reflected in small segments of time—flirting with them at the shopping mall? How did the big patterns, say the myths of mankind, relate to their smaller-scale cousins in real life? How much similarity did different patterns have to have to have beneficial resonance when they came into being side by side? Wasn't the latter the real basis for love? Isn't the creating of such patterns the basis of Art—real Art, which is making your life into an aesthetic expression? Isn't creating such patterns the true Will to Power?

If that line of reasoning was true, he hadn't fulfilled his pattern in his first marriage. He hadn't made it into Art.

The two books together had an eerie resonance. It would seem that "Changing perception" that Cassutto had wanted so much in 1904 had got a shot in the arm with the extension of human intelligence that computers represented.

It was about the time John Reynman had that thought that someone knocked loudly at his front door. He went to look through his peephole; there were three men dressed in black. This wasn't exactly the myth he was looking for in his life; he wanted something classier than UFO myths, but as Munchower argued, you took the Unknown in whatever form it came and you made Art out of it. She was big on CAPITALS as well.

He opened the door.

The three men were white, and their suits were actually a dark charcoal gray. Black ties, white shirts, black shades, clean-cut, a little too pasty, John decided.

"Good afternoon, are you Mr. John Reynman?"

"Yes, I am. And you are?"

"Here to talk with you sir, about your recent dealings with the Austin police. I think you'll find we are bringing good news."

All John could think of was the word "Gospel," which his Sunday school teacher had told him meant good news. Well he was ready for salvation now. He was tired of doing it all himself. Maybe the CIA, or whatever this was in front of him, could make his life into art. Celestial Intervention Agency.

He beckoned them in.

"Can I get your guys anything? Coke?"

"We're fine, unless you have some ice water."

That remark scared John. The summer before he went to school he had worked his butt off trying to sell magazine subscriptions door to door. The work was awful in the Texas heat. You had to say you were just points away from winning a trip to Europe, and when you were invited in the people's houses there were a couple of lines that were supposed to sell the magazines really well. One of them was claiming to be an orphan; the other was to ask for ice water. You see, ice water was pure, but it also subtly reminded the mark that you had been working your young clean-cut ass off in the heat selling these magazines. Who could say no to such a demonstration of youth and virtue? He was tempted to tell these guys that he was sorry that their fathers had all died.

He got the ice water.

"So what is the good news?"

The three men took turns speaking, but their lack of personality made it hard for John to remember which was which.

"We know that you are very interested in the death of Taylor Keziah Mason."

"I had been mildly curious."

When they didn't smile, John learned something. He realized that he couldn't give them any respect. Now they might hold the power of life and death over him, but he couldn't empower them any more by giving them any respect. He was amazed that after years of designing games this had finally hit him.

"We are fairly sure that you had nothing to do with his death."

"I could have told you that."

"We are very interested in Mason. In his papers, his effects, his thoughts. He was quite the mathematician. We hope that no one is investigating him."

"Investigating? Who are you?"

"We could show you FBI badges, but you know who we are."

"Scully and Muldoon?"

"Our names are no matter. We're here to tell you that no investigation will come from the local police if you are very, very quiet. You can get back to designing that game that is overdue. You can even date that round-heeled lawyer you've got."

"You guys sound pretty good at investigating things, so why don't you know more about Mason's death? What are you going to tell his family?"

"Mason died of a self-inflicted gunshot after months of strange behavior."

"Like looking like me. I do that all the time and I don't think it's strange, but you probably mean the people he hung out with."

"The Brotherhood of Ahasuerus. Yes, we'd like to know more about them. There's plenty of every form of oddness in Austin. Can you tell me more?"

Well that gamble had paid off.

John said, "Oh nothing much. Could you give me a phone number in case I find out anything?"

"If you talk in a phone anywhere, we know."

"Well that certainly makes things easy for me, doesn't it?"

"We'd much rather you not look into this any further."

"Of course not, I'm just a simple game designer, what do I know from mystical brotherhoods and dead mathematicians. Hey, I write about this stuff, I don't live it."

"Good. We thought you would feel that way. You keep quiet and everything will return to its natural course. Now do any of your neighbors know about the events?"

John didn't think the guy across the street could take this. "No," he replied.

"Your gaming group?"

"I hinted to them I might need an alibi, but I could tell them I was sleeping with a married woman."

"Good. We've already talked with your lawyer."

This wasn't fun. He had to take a deep breath and remind himself not to give these guys any respect; he had to view them as objects and himself as the subject.

"And she's agreeable?"

"Sure, she seems like the type that would agree with anything."

John collected the cold water glasses. When he came back to the living room they were all standing.

"It's been very nice getting to know you, Mr. Reynman."

"Drop by next time you're in the neighborhood."

"We may just do that."

Off to their black Lincoln and away.

After they turned off, he counted twenty-four and then walked to the convenience store and called Michelle. He figured they were good, but probably not good enough to monitor calls from just any phone.

While he waited to get through to her desk, a kid spilled part of a red slush drink on him.

"Hi hon, how was office life today?"

"You know you'll be getting a bill for the time I had to spend with the zombie triplets."

"Isn't that covered by love and devotion?"

"I'm a lover all right, but I'm still a lawyer. Jeez I felt like I needed to shower."

"So what do you think?"

"Well I don't think you need a lawyer right now."

John sighed. "But I sure as shit still need a lover."

"You romantic devil, you."

"You interested in buying me dinner?"

"Why should I buy you dinner?"

"You're billing me for the afternoon, remember?"

"Oh that's right. You going to be a good boy and leave things alone?"

John sighed again. "Like hell. I've slept through too many alarm clocks in my life. This may be a good time for you to move on, though. I mean I like you too much in case things do get bad."

"I've put up with bad before. See you at six."

John walked back home. Ahasuerus, Ahasuerus, now he knew that game, er, name. No, game. That was it! A friend of his who did some programming for whatsit, that create-a-civilization game, put in Ahasuerus as an Easter egg, unauthorized content that gamers love to look for and companies have a hate/love relationship with. Aviary Servin, that guy in San Francisco he had met at BuzzCon one year. Aviary, now why was the guy named after birds? Something about his mother's family being famous Italian bird-catchers. Anyway Aviary programmed in this old man who comes up and talks to the player, sort of mocking his achievements. Some immortal guy. The Wandering Jew. That was it, the Wandering Jew. He made fun of the players' lack of purpose, "Volitionary Ineptitude." John had been delighted with the phrase, wanting to spring it on people for weeks. Aviary later lost his job because of gay activism. He put some hunky gay men as background in one of the games instead of the cyber-bimbos he was supposed to create. He liked losing the job though; it gave him time to go back to his fiction. Aviary had told him that if you don't do what you're supposed to, you don't do very well. Sort of the Joseph Campbell "Follow your bliss" dictum. Aviary's little experimental books had done well as far as such things go—he'd been compared to Donald Barthelme and Dew D. Bon's *Cellophane Fawn* novels. So the Brotherhood of the Wandering Jew. John wondered if the Jew wandered around as much as John's mind did. Now that would be a hell of thing to try to model a brotherhood on, the meandering of the mind. It would have to be in constant travel, first this nook and then that.

Maybe Mason was just trying to stop the train, looking for a place to get off. John thought his life was pretty calm, would be a nice place for someone to get off, settle down, and not think too hard.

But John wasn't too sure he wanted that anymore.

No, he was becoming very sure he didn't want it anymore.

He went to a cheap Chinese place with Michelle. Over the number 3 dinner, Roast Duck With Bone In over rice, he asked her why she was interested.

"I told you. I love you, or at least I think I am beginning to love you," she said.

"Well what does that mean?"

"I don't know why I am interested. If I knew it would be less interesting."

"Love is a black thing, it is unknown because it is only from the unknown that we can make ourselves. Mystery is a spring of energy."

"That's great, a little flowery but great. Who said it?"

"Well I think John Fowles said the last part, but Cassilda said the first part."

"Do you think quoting your first wife is an aide to romantic intercourse?"

"We're not having intercourse, we're just talking. How do you like the duck?"

"The duck is great as always," sighed Michelle. "What are you going to do with the information you have?"

"Well one, I want to see if I can go after this academically or if somebody is still trying to kill me or scare me. I don't think I mind being scared, but I do mind being killed."

"And how do you think you'll determine this?"

"Well I'll see if any more bullets fly by me."

"Presuming that's over, then what?"

"Well the zombie trio mentioned the Brotherhood of Ahasuerus, so I thought I'd look into them, read those books that Mason was reading, see if I can find out more about Dr. Niles— I'm pretty sure he's the central mystery here. Maybe find out what Mason was doing (or did) if I can handle the math. I mean those guys were interested in him for some high-tech reason I'm sure."

"Does it occur to you that the three men told you that rather easily?"

"Well there goes my sense of being clever."

"They might want you to investigate things."

"Why would they want that?"

"Fools rush in where angels fear to tread."

"Does it worry you that you love a fool?"

"Fools can get better. It would worry me to love a hero. Only downhill from the start."

They walked to her car, and once again there was a gunshot.

Michelle fell, blood coming from her left temple.

While he was calling 911 inside the restaurant, and the old Chinese lady was helping Michelle to her feet, he knew he had to get her out of this. Whatever this was, it was more than the third time he was having to deal with bullets. It was worse.

They had hurt her.

And that was more important than anything else.

Get her safe.

Then hurt them back.

8 D. Niles and the Eternal Return

The guard didn't want to let John see Michelle. Well, it probably wasn't a question of want, it was probably some stupid regulation that involved gunshots. The police had already come, looked at John and left. Just plain looked at him, no explanation, no words of eternal vigilance, no forms to fill out. The guard was worse after that, so he tried the nurse, who offered to call back to the back and only assured John that her condition was "stable."

John hated the word "stable." "Stable" was only great when the status quo was working in your favor. When you were unhappy, the best thing to do was to change the status quo. You can't change yourself without changing the world. Change does not happen in a vacuum. He simply walked up to the guard and told him that he was going back there and if the guard wanted to, he could shoot him.

He walked around the guard. No bullets came, no threats or warning.

He found her in a curtained-off area. They had shaved her head just above her left ear and put a whopping big bandage on her scalp. She was alone. Why had they left her alone—didn't they know she had been shot?

"Hi, sweetie," he said.

"Hi," she said (with a little bit of a tremble in her voice).

"I didn't mean for this to happen," he said. "I guess it comes out of my bill."

"Guess so."

"So should I run up and kiss and squeeze, or treat you like fine china now?"

"You may kiss me very gently, right here," she said, tapping her left cheek.

He did so.

"I didn't want this to happen. I'll give it up. I'll stop it, but I won't let it happen again."

"John—"

"I have got to stop it; if I could, I would take that wound off your head and stick it on my own. I didn't know that something like this would happen."

"John, first off it's a small wound. It didn't even ring my bells. Well, not much."

"It's a fucking gunshot. You were shot because you were close to me. First they shoot someone in my house, then they shoot Dr. Niles's car, and now they shoot you."

"Chill. Whoever is after you is obviously a bad shot. That automatically puts you in a better class than Kennedy or Lennon."

"No one's ever suffered because of me."

"That's dumb. People always suffer because of other people's actions."

There was nothing to say to that.

"So how bad is it?" asked John.

"I'm going home tonight. It's nothing. You can drive me home. I'll call in sick tomorrow. I think the firm has a program for being shot."

"I'll stop. I'll stop looking."

"Don't you think that's dumb? First off, if you're a marked man do you think your intentions matter? Your intentions won't matter to whoever is out to get you. Intentions matter only in the way they mold your perception."

"You seem pretty calm about all this."

"I'm tranquilized all to hell."

"It's got to be Dr. Niles. I mean I think it was his car. I'll have it out with him."

"What does that mean, kill him, beat him till he confesses?"

"Something. I mean I've spent the last decade of my life writing games, where people do these things all the time. I need to do this stuff now."

The doctor came and talked about treating the wound, keeping it clean and coming back for stitches. He drove her home. Despite her brave talk, John saw how she looked around the hospital parking lot, looking for some menace in the shadows. He spent the night on the couch.

The next day he was at the Lost Weekend when it opened, confronting Bildad for Niles's address, which was in a nice quiet neighborhood in Austin called Hyde Park. His house looked like any of the other houses, his trees looked like trees, his detached garage looked like any other detached garage. There was a swing on the porch just like his grandmother's house in Amarillo had. He rang the bell.

Dr. David Niles looked a little bleary-eyed.

"Mr. Mason? No, that's not right, you told me when you shot at my car—Mr. Reynman. What the hell kind of name is that, anyway? Come in, I'm making coffee."

"My girlfriend was shot last night."

"You're kind of a dangerous person to be around, aren't you? Is this a habit?" asked Dr. Niles.

John had followed him into his kitchen, where he was making coffee in a percolator. The house was strange, full of photos and paintings—in some places the art was so thick as to obscure even the smallest traces of wall. John had not meant to follow him into the kitchen, but the movements and mannerisms made by Dr. Niles made him do it, as if Dr. Niles were communicating directly to his body.

"Sit down, it will take the coffee a while," said Dr. Niles. "You know what I think? I think Vonnegut is right. He says Americans shoot each other so often because they are trying to live like characters in a storybook. Shooting is a great device to end a book or a story—it helps give people beginnings, middles, and ends."

"You think my girlfriend was shot because somebody read too many stories?"

"Well not like that. I don't ascribe to the idea that people are that media driven. Just because we may see a lot of comedy on the screen doesn't mean you'll start doing comedy in real life."

"You're a nut. I'm talking to a madman."

"I didn't come to your house at eleven in the morning to tell you my girlfriend was shot."

"I came because you know something."

"I know nothing."

"Your car was at my house when I found the body."

"The body of your girlfriend? Or another body?"

"The body of Mr. Mason."

"My God, man, you're an absolute path of carnage. If I worried for my safety I would throw you out right now—although disrupting the obligation of hospitality would be just as terrifying. I've got some cookies my neighbor baked. Would you like some with your coffee?"

"Why don't you fear for your safety?"

"Because I am a traveler. I am on a journey, and travel brings its own protection."

"You don't live here?"

"I live here. My journeys are no longer so obviously tourism. Once one learns that life is the process of traveling and then looking back over where you've been, a certain protection comes your way. There's a good fortune for travelers. So I teach travel."

"This isn't getting me anywhere."

"Where do you want to go?"

"I want people to stop shooting at Michelle."

"Well the first step would be to figure out why people are shooting at Michelle."

"They're shooting at Michelle because of me."

"And they're shooting at you because—"

"Because I know too much."

"Well now you see how much better off I am since I know nothing. What do you know?"

"I'm not telling you because I don't trust you."

"Isn't it a bad policy to eat and drink with people you don't trust? I could have poisoned the cookies or the coffee."

"I've seen you drink the coffee and eat the cookies."

"Are you sure you saw me eat a cookie?"

John panicked, and started to gag himself. Dr. Niles very deliberately picked a homemade chocolate chip cookie and ate it.

Dr. Niles said, "Don't you think it's a little odd that you would come to me, D. Niles, to discuss your problems, when you probably know better yourself?"

"I think you know something."

"Perhaps, Mr. Reynman, this is the first time you've acted in your life at some level beyond seeking pleasure and avoiding pain. Such action always makes life more meaningful, but leads to paranoia. Why don't you relax, ask questions, and enjoy your cookies."

The cookies, John suddenly noticed, were good.

"How did you know Mason?"

"He came to my lectures on the occult."

"He looked like me."

"A rather studied attempt, I must say. Your blond hair looks natural. I believe the first time I met Mr. Mason he had darker hair than you—seems he must have worked at getting it to be the same shade."

"So he wanted to look like me."

"Yes. A bad idea—oh don't get me wrong, you're good-looking enough. It's a bad idea to try to look like anyone else. The body is different than any other object. It is after all the only object we experience from the inside. To try and make your body look like another's is to reduce it to an object. The body, as I believe Merleau-Ponty is fond of pointing out, is the mediator between objective reality and subjective conscious-ness. If you reduce it to the objective pole, a certain madness will occur. How authentic a life can you have in someone else's body?"

"You think Mason was crazy?"

"He strikes me as inauthentic. Being is given by human experience; to accept the text of another is an affront to the self."

"Isn't that what most people do? I mean we dress, we eat, we do everything because of TV. It doesn't seem likely that you can reject all of it."

"Not without being a monk or a total eccentric. I tried both of those. I am still somewhat caught up in those two paths. No matter how far you travel, you've still got the same road behind you."

"Where did you travel to?"

"Places that are easy to imagine, like Kansas, and hard to imagine, like pre-sand Egypt. I went to Benares to sit in the biggest funeral pyre in the world. I lived in a small town in southern India called Malgudi. I have lived in Paris and New York and tiny towns in Iowa like Polk City. I traveled for lived experience that wasn't as culturally defined."

"But then you settled here."

"Oh I am not settled. I'll probably live in this delightful city till I die. Did you know that O. Henry called it the 'City of the Violet Crown'? A lovely name—I think we should all use that more often. No, I traveled until I learned how to do the process internally. If I were a tad more romantic I would call it Questing. Looking for the Holy Graal."

"What is the Graal?"

"It is anything and everything that you look upon with the Orpheus gaze. You know the story of Orpheus, how he went to hell to find his beloved, and was allowed to leave with her with the one taboo—he must not look upon her until they came into the bright air of this world? Well, he looks and she fades away from him. The Graal is like that. It is always fading away. It's like hearing the best music in the world and suddenly you realize that the concert is half over, the movie nearly done, the book a third of the way read. There is a sadness. Now if you can accept that sadness as part of the whole process of traveling you'll do amazing things. But it causes most people to spin out."

"Do you think that's what happened to Mason?"

"I am a photographer, not a psychologist. You found the body—what was his last emotion?"

John tried to picture the body again, trying to see its look. It looked like John thought he did when he was surprised.

"Surprised. He was surprised."

In fact John realized the body's expression and his would have been the same when he first saw it.

John said, "Wait a minute, this whole losing touch with your body as a way of going crazy, has that happened to me?"

"I doubt that there are any parameters of sanity for someone going through what you're going through. We don't have a lot of cultural analogs for what you're experiencing. I can't think of any mythic ones either. Maybe you're making a myth for the future."

"Pity there's not good pay in that."

"Oh maybe you'll meet a leprechaun that will grant wishes or some such."

"You believe in leprechauns too?"

"No I don't believe in them at all. I photographed one once in north Austin. Damnedest thing I ever saw when he showed up in the picture. Looked like Pan. I still don't know what to make of it. Don't suppose you have any advice?"

"I thought you were the teacher."

"I told you before, I know nothing. Well I do know it's time for you to go. I've got a photography class to teach at one and I'm going to the theater tonight—they're doing *The World and the Door*, one of O. Henry's plays. It's my favorite."

Later, as John was designing a scene between Sethos and a leprechaun in the forest, the body question came to mind. He couldn't believe he took for granted what Dr. Niles had said about the body as object being a type of insanity. Dr. Niles didn't seem like a real poster boy for sanity, but that made sense. It had the ring of truth. The thing he hadn't considered was the Electric Luddite tattoo. He was ashamed of it. When he made love to Clarissa he hid it. Maybe he had mentioned the tattoo to one or two gaming buds over the years, but he had never shown it to them. Only Cassilda had seen it, or his mom. That meant Mason had to have met them. In Amarillo. He would have to go there. His hometown held perhaps the roots of Mason's madness. What had molded him had molded the dead man. One authentic, one inauthentic and apparently subject to some kind of judgment thereby.

If he went home for a while, he could talk to Mom, maybe patch up something with Cassilda. Best of all, if *he* was the target for the shots fired at Michelle and Dr. Niles's car, they would be safe. But what about Mom?

Well it would take them a while to track him down. He could take his laptop and keep working, just show up and surprise her. He could go early tomorrow. There would be a Southwest jet leaving for Dallas and then on to Amarillo.

He didn't want to call Michelle—her phone could be tapped. He would post a letter, walk away from his house to get a cab, and then surprise Mom tomorrow afternoon. He still had a key to her house after all these years.

He printed out the letter.

> Dear Michelle,
> I can't endanger you by hanging around. I'm on my way to Shangri-La for a few days. I think you'll be safer and I'll have a chance to find out something that may change what I'm fighting. I love you. I need you to trust that I will find the truth of my quest. I'll be back. There's a special providence that looks after travelers.
>
> > Love,
> > (S.) John

He posted it from the downtown post office, the one nearest her apartment. He packed two suitcases and his laptop. In the cold predawn he walked to the convenience store and called for a cab.

9 Peanuts

Like most Texans John Reynman flew Southwest Airlines. It was cheap, cramped, and reliable, and they gave you a free soft drink (well half of one in a plastic cup), a bag of peanuts, and a cookie. Sometimes you didn't get the cookie. Peanuts were the emblem of the airline, signifying cheap fare. The airline had started in Dallas, and John would have a stopover there. The sun was coming up just as he took off and the airport was releasing a weather balloon that for a single silvery moment looked just like a saucer.

This was the first time in his adult life that John had flown without a book. He had always despised those people who didn't have enough respect for themselves to know to carry a book along. In fact John often rated folk by what carry-on books they took, from current rack-fodder to obscure things hunted down in dimly lit used-book stores and offering the secrets of the universe, or at least a good read.

He ate his peanuts and drank his Sprite, and planned his trip to Amarillo. He would just surprise Mom. Mom was seventy-six and lived in the house that John and Matthew had been born in.

Her health was good and John and his three brothers lived in a comforting illusion that her health would always be good. Few things (before the past few weeks) scared John as much as the idea that his mother might die. Who would know how to do anything? Dealing with lawyers and selling the house—was there some kind of service that took all of those things away? It seemed to John that he should know these things. He was in his late thirties—didn't you know everything by the time you were in your thirties? His parents had known. He had expected them to know everything. He had even thought of calling his mother about the double, but imagined that was beyond her expertise.

Now he would need a cover story for visiting Mom. Oh shit, how long was he going to visit? A day, a week, or just hide there the rest of his life? He couldn't imagine any kind of harm coming to him at his mother's house. It had always seemed secure in all ways. Mom and Dad were both one-marriage people, living through poverty and good times, sickness and health, Dad's drinking. No one had that strength anymore.

He would tell Mom that he needed a break from the creative life. Not that she viewed being the designer of electronic games as creative. He would tell Mom that he was researching a game to be set in Amarillo, something to do with Pantex, where they store the plutonium, and the helium plant where his grandfather had worked, and those weird signs Stanley Marsh 3 was putting up around the city, and it could all have a climax in Palo Duro Canyon. It would have a whole level based on the Oprah trial.

In Dallas he bought a book for the rest of the trip. It was *Power Speak* by Ross DiBrehl, one of those manuals of meta-communications that suggests if you just use certain words and certain tones you will automagically get people to do your will. Inspired by the title alone, John asked for and received double peanuts, and as a further act of rebellion didn't eat them. Ross explained,

> "The secret is to speak of things as though they have already happened. There is a power in the past tense, a form of believability. If you tell yourself every day that you will live long and prosper, you will live long. If you tell everyone that you have prospered you will do so. People long to fill out the past, because they are afraid of the anxiety that comes from not having words and reality match up. That's the hocus-pocus that lets storytelling take place."

Ross went on like this for pages, but it was magic enough to let the time pass and find himself at the airport ordering a cab.

The flight had taken all day. It was only a couple of hours in the air, but it was the layover in Dallas that had done it. There isn't much of a fall in Amarillo and the October colors aren't pretty. He saw some of the Dynamite Museum signs. They looked like real road signs but carried surrealist messages. They were the brainchildren of Stanley Marsh 3, the Amarillo eccentric who had paid the Ant Farm to install Cadillac Ranch—buried Cadillacs not far from the helium plant. The signs looked like yellow Yield signs; his mother had told him that each sign cost Stanley nearly five hundred dollars. The signs read:

The Earth is an Airport. Catch your Flight

Road Does Not End

and the third sign had an image of the Mona Lisa on it.

Close into town after the cab had turned off I-40, he saw a sign with an image of a triceratops and the word CROSSING written below.

When Cadillac Ranch had had its twentieth anniversary,

Stanley had given a party. He had the Cadillacs spray-painted white. John had snagged an invite because one of the Ant Farm members was interested in game development. John had taken his mom. It had been the third year of his divorce from Cassilda. Stanley had given everyone spray paint cans and told them to write what they wanted on the cars. At first John's mom refused, but then asked to write something. She wrote the name of her grade school—Soncy. She had gone to Soncy School, a rural school whose ruins could be seen from the Cadillac Ranch. Her family had sharecropped for the family of Mr. Marsh's wife. John wondered what she would have thought when she learned her letters just so few hundreds yards away—to use them to write graffiti on a car planted in the ground (at the angle of the Great Pyramid in Egypt) on North Solstice sixty-one years later. Something too strange in that. America's Stonehenge.

The old neighborhood hadn't changed. He tipped the cabbie and braced himself to tell lies to his mother. He had been telling lies to his mother for years; after all he had gone to college, and it is the nature of higher education in America to learn to lie well.

He rang the bell, and waited till he was scared.

You get scared when your mother is seventy-six.

He took the key from his pocket. He had had the key since Mom gave it to him in junior high. He went in yelling.

He hadn't thought of her not being there. On Thursdays she had Bible study, and on Sundays she went over to one of her high school friends (Amarillo High class of '39) and watched football—mainly the Cowboys.

He went to his old room.

It was a couple of hours before dark, and he knew that she would be home before dark. After Dad had died, she never went anywhere after dark. She said it made her afraid. He spent many hours trying to get her to face this fear. But after a while he had accepted it.

He turned on his old TV—it had been bought in the year of the American Bicentennial—and flipped from channel to channel, waxing nostalgic at what a big deal it was when they got cable. Mom often waxed about the night they got electric power out at the farm near Soncy. They had a bulb in every room. All four of them. Just a bare bulb hanging from a wire. They had waited till it was real dark, then hit the lights, and spent all night just walking from room to room and watching the miracle. They had seen electricity, of course. It was the rule in town, but not on the farm. They were progressive, part of the modern age.

Mom got electricity the same year Georgia O'Keeffe taught art at the Teacher's College in nearby Canyon, Texas.

None of the shows were good.

It got dark, and John was scared.

He called up one of his aunts and asked if she knew where Mom was, he didn't explain he was in town.

No idea, Aunt Sally said.

John didn't know the name of her friend she watched football with.

The shows didn't get any more interesting. He tried reading more *Power Speak*. It advocated never listening too closely to anyone's sorrows lest you be drawn into the "rhythms of negativity." John kept thinking of Mom's dictum, "Everyone has a story that will break your heart." And he began to worry that she might be having a real problem. He could picture her at the hospital—where they were desperately calling his home in Austin. He turned off the light in his old room and lay in his old bed trying to be calm and rational.

The bed, or more specifically the smell of the laundry detergent that Mom still used after all these years, triggered memories of his favorite fantasies. These involved saving people—usually men he thought of as great thinkers or writers in his teenage years. Some illiterate thug—probably a Christian fundamentalist—would be menacing, say, Dr. Isaac Asimov. John had had a real crush on the idea of psychohistory. Anyway, this gun-toting thug would be menacing Asimov, probably due to the latter's atheism, and then John would call attention to himself. "What's up Doc?" he'd say, and the non sequitur would mesmerize the slow-witted cad. John would then quickly slap the gun from the miscreant's hand and gain the attention and admiration of Dr. Asimov. This would lead to a dual career in organic chemistry and science fiction writing—both paths to power that John lusted after in his geeky high school days. Where had that courage gone? Even in his fantasies, courage was gone. He was going to lie in this pool of courage and soak it up. Somewhere along the line adults lose their courage. If he had only had it when he had been married to Cassilda, he would still be married to her. He imagined the courage as sort of a dark blue shining pool around his body and let it soak in. It was easy for it to soak in, there being such a need for it in his current life—and such an abundance of it in his teenage years. Courage is easy when you have overprotective parents. It was a warm and soothing thought, and passed into dream.

He was in some kind of vast hall. He was giving a lecture. He stood before two large blackboards covered in mathematical symbols. He couldn't make out the audience—the hall was dark—but he knew there were many, many people watching him, waiting for him to explain his result. He had had it a minute ago. It was so simple. So easy to grasp. It was the meaning of life, and he was going to explain it. He knew that if he could be left alone for a few minutes longer, he would have it again. Remember. Just remember it. But the crowd wasn't patient. They began to hiss and to throw things. Ice cubes. They were throwing ice cubes from their drinks. They were hailing him to death. The ice got whiter and smaller, but it stung more. If they would just stop . . .

The sound of a car pulling into the driveway awakened him.

He needed to think. He didn't want to scare Mom. He had better go out and meet her before she put the car away. He knew she was afraid of the dark.

He ran to the side door.

It wasn't Mom's car. It was a sports utility vehicle.

A man was getting out.

John ran through his mom's house quickly, to her bedroom to get Dad's gun. It hadn't been fired in eighteen years, but it was still a gun. If they had found him, he had Dad's snub-nosed .38. He ran back to the front room of the house and hid his body behind Dad's recliner. When the door opened he would be hidden from the opener.

The door opened. It was his mother, followed by a gray-haired gentleman. As soon as they stepped in the dining room, they kissed. Mom laughed and headed away from John into the kitchen. The short gray-haired man followed. He seemed so old. Far too old for Mom—hell he must *be* her age. Well that was far too old. Dad's hair had been silver. Pure, and it along with his meerschaum pipe became icons of maturity for John. John still found himself thinking that he was dealing with a wise man whenever he smelled Sir Walter Raleigh pipe tobacco. Of course this was perhaps not the time to be critiquing Mom's new boyfriend.

She was making coffee. He should go just go in and introduce himself. But why had she not told him? He believed that Mom had never hidden anything from him ever. She even called him when her lawnmower needed fixing, as though his maleness somehow gave him an insight into the problems of all mechanical things.

So he moved swiftly through the dark dining room to the door of the kitchen. He would announce himself at the appropriate time. He wanted to hear what was being discussed in the kitchen.

The gray-haired man had a son and a daughter. The daughter was having marriage troubles, the son owned a dry-cleaning firm. Mom said nice things about John's brothers. The twins were doing fine, Matthew still wasn't talking to her. Well, that wasn't news. John was the odd one, he did something with computers. The gray-haired man worried about his daughter's ability to support herself. She had been some sort of secretary before she had married her jerk husband. John realized that she must be in her forties. Mom talked about what a good marriage John had had, how sad she was that it had broken up. If Mom had only known the kind of things that Cassilda was into.

Their talk became silly, there were pauses. John realized that they must be making out. Maybe he should go outside and wait for the gray-haired man to leave. He could come up then, explain he had just flown into town on a whim. No, he would have to call her—Mom didn't open her doors at night. Well Mom may have an entire set of behavior that he didn't know about.

They got up, and the light under the kitchen door went out. John sprinted back to the front room to hide behind his father's chair, but then he realized that the couple was heading back to Mom's bedroom.

He hoped they wouldn't see the open drawer with the gun missing.

Surely they weren't going to have sex.

John went to his bedroom. Mom didn't use that room at all, so he could wait it out. At least he couldn't hear anything.

He took the gun out of his pocket.

It's hard to tell time without a watch, but he realized that at least an hour must have passed. Maybe the guy was going to spend the night.

That meant John should sneak out of here and show up tomorrow. It would be a long walk to a place where he could catch a cab—he didn't think he could call one without them hearing his voice.

He would just have to wait. He pushed open one of the windows. It was too cold to be thinking of sleeping outside, but he managed to set both suitcases and his laptop outside. Come dawn he would slip out—maybe go down to that doughnut place that he remembered as still being open during his last visit to see Mom three years ago.

The idea of doughnuts made him hungry, so he opened his peanuts, both packs, and ate them one by one to make them last.

When the sky got a little bit light, he crawled out the window, and began making his way to the doughnut shop.

It was cold as hell. In Austin, unlike Amarillo, October mornings don't mean frost. He just hoped that nobody would turn him in as part of the neighborhood watch. The frost melted a little and made his shoes wet.

He could've left one of the suitcases in the closet, damn it. It was eight blocks to the doughnut place. The waitress, the two cops, and the black man on his way to work looked at him like he had just come in from Mars. The cops didn't approach or anything. Maybe they've seen guys that sleep in their clothes, and carry two suitcases and a laptop into doughnut stores at 5:45 A.M.

He realized that he was still carrying Dad's gun.

He ordered a couple of chocolate-glazed doughnuts and a cup of coffee. He opened one suitcase and removed *Power Speak* from it—he had stashed it there at the airport. He couldn't find a chapter on dealing with cops in doughnut shops and loaded guns. Maybe past tense will help, he decided grimly.

He read, he ate doughnuts, he drank coffee. He tried like hell to be invisible. The cops left, the shift changed, and he felt a little safer when he was finally the person who had been in the shop the longest.

At eight he called Mom and told her that he had flown into town, and was dropping by.

She sounded fine and bright. She was looking forward to seeing him. Nothing about "Wait till my lover leaves" or "John, I've got a surprise for you."

He waited half an hour before he called a cab, so it would take him long enough to have arrived from the airport.

Mom met him at the door. No one else was at the house.

He put his suitcases in his room again, noticed the two peanut bags on the floor.

Later, when Mom was in the bathroom, he returned Dad's gun to its drawer. Someone had closed the drawer in the night.

10 Dry Ice and Texas Heat

Mom bought all of his explanations, or perhaps simply seemed uninterested. She asked how long he meant to stay and seemed a little troubled by the lack of a definite answer.

She had to go shopping since she didn't have food for two. For the first time ever in all his trips home, she didn't ask him to go with her. Stay and unpack, she said.

John guessed that she had to call the gray-haired man. He wondered if he had woken them up, or perhaps he slipped away at the dawn. John was mad at himself for being bothered by the whole thing. He had better get with the program if he wanted to hide out here awhile.

After he unpacked he began going through his things. John always left stuff at Mom's. It was a kind of insurance against her death. She couldn't die as long as he left stuff. The oldest boys, the twins, didn't come here at all, or maybe one visit every seven years, which was nothing. They were older and therefore more scared of death. Matthew, the youngest, had broken relations with Mom when she had made an off-color remark about his black wife Haidee—Haidee's murder last year had no doubt made the rift permanent. John found a yellow spiral notebook. He had started it during his marriage with Cassilda. He had been tinkering with the idea of becoming a novelist. Like many game designers he had written a work-for-hire novel that was keyed to a game system. *Palace of Mirrors* had been set in a postholocaust Greenland, which he called Zembla. He had tried to write a novel on his own at Cassilda's urging.

There was a novel beginning "Many years later when he faced the mad gunman Gary Paragorian would remember the day his father showed him dry ice." John had been very much under the spell of García Márquez at that time—Cassilda had introduced him to *One Hundred Years of Solitude*. John had hoped to write a magical realist novel set in Amarillo and Austin. He remembered the day his father had shown him dry ice.

Dad was a warehouseman. He was director of operations of a food warehouse that supplied mom-and-pop groceries from Dallas to Denver. One day, John must've been about seven, his dad showed him a big white loaf wrapped in brown paper on the train dock of the warehouse. Smoke was coming off into the hot Texas night. "That's dry ice. Don't touch it, it burns."

As soon as Dad was away, John touched it. It burned like hell.

Dad came back in a moment.

"Burned like hell, didn't it?" asked Dad. Dad had some gloves on and lifted the dry ice onto a wagon and moved it into the freezer—a huge vast cold room. Years later it still amazed John how sure Dad had been that he had touched it. He felt that he couldn't be as sure of human behavior. Maybe that was why he always went for jobs that required as little human interaction as possible. His gaming buddy Mark had a friend who was getting a master's degree in psychology. As part of the training he had to counsel psychotics (or as they called them these days, people with Anti Social Disorders). He was supposed to get them working in jobs that made use of their brains, but kept them from interacting with the public. One of the recommended jobs was working for the post office. John always took great joy in this fact, and seldom passed a postman on the street without thinking, *I could have been a great postal carrier.*

Then John remembered that he had had this notebook when Cassilda and he had gone to that Electric Luddite concert where he had dropped acid and decided to get the tattoo. He had, he found paging through the book, designed the tattoo in this notebook. Yeah there it was. What a goddamn ugly thing. Underneath were his notes about the gig:

"Ned Ludd, probably not a real person at all, a VR person maybe based on Ned Luddlam, bad rap. They didn't reject technology as technology, they revolted against the poverty caused by the American Nonintercourse act. Their revolt was centered on politics and economics—but that was something the state didn't want us to know about, so the fictional leader became a thick-browed technology hater.

"The Band is so cool. They have this black bus like the photo negative of the bus that Ken Kesey drove and Saul and Paul saw in 1964. They had all the luck that year—they got to hear Richard and Mimi Farina, too. The guitarist is Joe Morbid. A fat, muscular, blond young man in ragged, tight black jeans and a loose, dirty, polyester black T-shirt. He walks in a cloud of smoke. He knows the difference between hating technology and hating bad social programs. He's going to teach this to the world.

"He's with this chick, a dishwater blonde dressed in a thousand black and midnight blue ribbons. I think she's in love with Cassilda. Her name is Mary Denning and she sells decals after the show that read 'Wouldn't I taste better?' They're holster decals. For guns.

"The other chick, the one that's in the band, is Sally Sabotage. She talked to me about all sorts of peaceful resistance. She wrote their hit 'Burrito Zapata.'

"The first step will be that we will all get Electric Luddite tattoos. It will be a sign of the end of blind obedience to authority. Then we'll all start writing FNORD on the back of dollar bills. When the day comes that you go to the bank and you take out a hundred dollar bills and twenty of them have FNORD written on them we can begin the revolution.

"Mostly we do act and we do not go mad—now *that's* mystery."

John remembered leaving the concert and looking for a tattoo parlor. He had taken the acid about half an hour before the concert. Cassilda didn't trip. She didn't believe in it. She thought people were fucked-up enough not to need extra distraction. She had got them backstage somehow, and he remembered in a strange distorted way having long talks about politics with Joe Morbid, who seemed sharper than the average guy—of course the acid made the cover of the yellow spiral notebook pretty damn interesting too. Joe's big point was that everyone could have a lot more freedom in his or her life if they simply took it. This was pretty much Cassilda's take. Looking back on it, Cassilda's bisexuality was already evident too in her reaction to Mary Denning. She was probably planning on a threesome—figuring that the acid would open him enough for some changes. But the idea of revolution was semiotic; John would become a symbol of the revolution.

Maybe he would've got somewhere if the tattoo was some-place people could see it. The upper arm is so easily covered.

He had followed the Electric Luddites for a couple of years afterward. The band faded away. It never really made it big, not even with "Burrito Zapata." They had tried a lot of strange stuff, like recording sounds of various hate groups and playing them back mixed with Muzak outside of shopping malls. Sounds of conditioning too—like the sounds you hear from your phone as you're waiting for the call to go through. They gave classes on sound and its use. They taught rune galdor and vowel songs. But they never quite fit into the occult world, just as they never fit into the rock 'n' roll world. He hadn't heard of them playing a gig in years. Mason had to have known Cassilda or one of the ex-members.

John had sold both of their albums long ago.

Maybe the whole thing was political. That would make the interest of the federal government clear. The Electric Luddites always insisted that they weren't in favor of overthrowing the government, they were interested in people simply being freer under our present regime. "People give away their freedom. People have forgotten their own better natures. Kill the warder in the mirror first, the others will follow later."

Suddenly John regretted that he hadn't taken their advice and written FNORD on the back of all of his dollar bills. The warder-in-the-mirror quote suddenly froze John. After all, he had seen his mirror image, but he hadn't killed him. Unless of course some weird programming had made him rise up out of his sleep and kill Mason. It made as much sense as anything. Who knows what had gone down while he was on acid four-teen years ago? Could he have been programmed to kill his mirror image that long ago?

He remembered buying the acid. Cassilda and he had gone

back to Amarillo to see the concert. The Electric Luddites were playing cities like Amarillo, Texas, and Becky's Ham, New Mexico, but bypassing Austin and Dallas. Cassilda must have known someone in the band—how else would she have known about such an obscure concert? Anyway, they were staying at his mom's and they decided to walk by John's old high school campus, where this guy approached them and told them he was out of money and if he could just sell a sheet of blotter he could make bus fare. He offered to let them try a hit each, and then if they liked they could buy the sheet. John said no, but asked how much one hit would cost. Four dollars. What an odd amount, you'd have to make change and everything. But as it turned out he had exactly four ones in his pocket. He thought Cassilda would be pleased, proud of his rebel ways, but she just commented on the fatefulness of having the exact change. It was one of her "magical" remarks that he never knew if she was being serious or just yutzing around. Probably she didn't either.

He had agreed to let her drive to the concert. He remembered her telling his mother that they would be back late, BECAUSE SHE KNEW SOMEONE IN THE BAND. That's right.

He would have to get hold of her and find out about the connection between the Electric Luddites and Mason.

He paged through the yellow notebook some more—perhaps he had written something else useful.

There was a list of Electric Luddite tunes from the concert:

The Way Out
Burrito Zapata
The Maze of Fear and Doubt
Smash the Clocks
Mirror Men from Mars
Meme Sabotage

The President's Slurpee

The Yellow Sign

Bitches and Bikes

The first title made him more than a little queasy. Was it connected with the book he'd found in Mason's car? Damn, that song had been on one of the albums. He had heard it for years. Now think. Something about Dreamsicles. No, that made no sense. No. Yes. Dreamsicles. That was right, something about Dreamsicles. He had asked Joe Morbid about it, and . . . Damn it. He had asked Joe Morbid about it—was it some kind of hidden message telling everyone to take some sort of drug? Joe had looked at him with the greatest "you loser" look and told him that drugs were part of the control structure. All drugs. People who think that they're rebelling by smoking, snorting, injecting X, Y, or Z serve the same god as the people with their six-packs or who watch their church shows on TV. The god of distraction. They wouldn't get the song. No, damn it, how did it go? It was kind of scary. John knew that he had listened to the song while working for years in the early eighties churning out game reviews. Now it was lost to him, probably a victory for the god of distraction.

He remembered how horrified his mom had been by the tattoo. She wanted him to promise that he would never tell any of her friends. He was something of a trailblazer, he realized. Now in the late nineties, many men and women of his class and age had got tattoos to stave off the coming of age. But they would find as he had found that age cannot be staved off. Learning that is one of the few truths we really have available to us as human beings.

The front doorbell rang.

John peeked from the curtain in his room.

It was Mrs. Hahn from next door, a tiny bent woman with

hair as white as snow. He had hated her as a child because she was old. She must be older than dirt now.

He decided to answer the door.

"Oh John, why are you here? Are things as bad as that?"

"Hello, Mrs. Hahn. What are you talking about?"

"Your mother's hiatal hernia. I knew she was going to have surgery on it soon, but I didn't think this soon. Were the other tests bad?"

"What other tests? I don't know what you're talking about."

"You are here because of her health, aren't you?"

"No, I needed to do some research on Palo Duro Canyon for a game I'm designing."

"You're old enough to stop with games I think. You're here taking up your mother's time because of a game when she's practically dying?"

"I had no idea."

"Oh that's just like Elaine," said Mrs. Hahn. "Never tell anyone, never bother anyone, just quietly go off to the grave."

"She seemed fine last night," said John.

"Of course she did, the problem comes in the night, she has to retch her food up you know. It's very painful. It's hereditary too. The twins already have it, you're probably next. Every night—it must be awful."

"When did all this start?"

"She's had it for years, ever since your father died. I thought the world of your father. Every night I thank God for Him having let me know two such good men, Dominic and your father."

Dominic was the late Mr. Hahn. Mom had suggested that he had been talked to death.

John asked, "How did you know about it?"

"Well heavens, doesn't the light come on in her bathroom every night at three-thirty sharp? So one day I asked her what was the problem, and she told me that she had a hiatal hernia, and I told her then, 'You'd better get that seen to,' but did she, oh no, not on your life, you know how she is, never talks to any-body, never takes any advice, nothing like that, and so it went on and on and now she's going to have surgery because if you let those things go you wind up in surgery. I told her but no, and now those other tests."

By this time Mrs. Hahn had sat in the chair covered in gold crushed velvet. John had strayed midway into the front room, trying to get his bearings.

"What are the other tests, Mrs. Hahn?"

"Oh I don't know, tests. Cancer probably. We have a very high rate of cancer here because of the plutonium in the water. Much higher than anywhere else."

"When did she get these tests?"

"Why just last Friday, that's why I thought you were here, because of her health. I mean my children would be with me if I were getting tests."

"Your children still live with you, don't they?"

"My point exactly."

"Can I get you something to drink, some coffee?"

"Oh heavens no, I am far too busy for that. I just needed to stop by and find out about Elaine's tests. There are people wait-ing to know. I find these things out. Otherwise nobody would ever know anything. Heavens knows that Elaine never tells anybody anything. She's worried that it would scare you kids. Hell you're thirty-eight, the twins are fifty-two. Matthew is thirty-five. Old enough to know. You know what her biggest fear is?"

"No ma'am."

"Her biggest fear is that she will die and people will find her lying in her house days after she's gone. She's afraid that news would be traumatic for you boys. She asked me to come by every few days to see that she's not dead. One day you boys will be getting a call from me. 'Elaine's dead,' I'll say. 'I found her.' So you needn't worry. I am screwing up my courage every day just to find a body. Can you imagine what that would be like?"

"No, ma'am. Not at all."

11 Confessions and Heavy Metal

During the rich golden sunlight of late afternoon John got his mother to talk about her health. He had dropped hints all morning.

She had a hiatal hernia. No, she didn't throw up every night, just most nights. She knew Herman had waited too long to go to a doctor. Herman's father had been a doctor and he had felt that all good doctoring skill had died with him. She was scared she had waited too long. She hadn't told the boys. They would just worry. She had spent many years of her adult life worrying about her parents. The worry hadn't done them any good, and it wouldn't do her any good. And that was the end of it.

"When are you going to have your surgery?"

"Next month, November," she said.

"Were you even going to tell me at all?"

"I was going to mention it. You might have called and then you would have worried that I wasn't home. I'm sure you boys picture me as always being home. I've got a life, you know."

"I just never thought you kept anything from us."

"Being an adult means keeping some things from other adults. It is a question of borders."

"But some borders are meant to be crossed. We wouldn't have any travel without borders being crossed."

"Aren't you supposed to be working on a game? I had hoped that we could go to Palo Duro Canyon tomorrow. You had said your game took place there, so I figured it would help you to check out the canyon. I invited a friend along, Henry Crawford."

"Who's he?"

"A man in my walking group, although I first met him in Bible study. Minor prophets."

John heard that as "minor profits" and figured the man was secondary to what she had gained in Bible study. There's always the little things you gain from a bigger study. Not only does one question lead to ten more questions, but it leads to neat side benefits as well.

John announced that he was going to work on his game, but first he wanted to take a drive. Could he borrow Mom's car?

She geased him to put gas in the car and he was gone. He didn't want to call Michelle from his mom's house in case there was some kind of monitoring of her phone.

He called from Sunset Center Mall. Mom had some kind of history with the owner of the mall, she had doubled-dated with him or something. Anything old enough Mom had some kind of history with, but the buildings in question were always "new" to her.

He got Michelle at her office. She wasn't happy.

"I thought," she said, "that you were dead, and when I figured out that your message was legit I kind've wished you were."

"I had to get out of there, someone was trying to kill me," he said.

"What about me?"

"You're why I left—I was afraid that you would get hurt. I can't fight some invisible conspiracy. You're safe. I mean, you are safe, aren't you?"

There was a long pause and John became aware of a balding man in a black trench coat who was visiting one of the little antique shops. He looked a little like Dr. Niles.

She finally said, "Well I'm a little scared. Last night I heard someone walking down the hall in front of my apartment, and I thought maybe it was you. I tiptoed to the door and looked out the peephole. It was a small dark-haired woman, maybe an Indian. She had walked up to my door and was just staring at it. It was three in the morning. You don't just stare at someone's door at three in the morning. I didn't know what to do. She wasn't carrying a gun or anything, unless it was in her purse. She just stood there. I didn't want to make a sound by walking back to phone the police. After a while she just left. I had the weird feeling that she knew I was there."

"Did you call the police then?"

"I went to watch the parking lot. She drove off in a little red car like yours."

"Then you called the police."

"And report that someone stood in front of my door?"

"Yes, exactly, that's suspicious behavior."

"You think the police are going to look into door staring?"

"You've got to do something."

"Like run off to Mama?"

The balding man had left the antique shop and was walking toward the phones.

"I don't know what to do. Should I come back?"

"Come back when you're ready to be a man about things, or don't come back at all."

"None of this sounds like you."

"How the hell do you know what I sound like—because you've slept with me a couple of times? I'm ready to put my life on the line for you because I thought you were in a place nobody had been before. You seemed so different. You went with me to visit my dad. Now you're heading back to your past."

The balding man had begun to make a call at the phone next to John's. John wished for the phone booths of yore—all encased in safety glass and aluminum. What the hell were the designers thinking when they left you as exposed as this?

"I'm not heading back to my past. Well maybe I am, but only to pick up a few things that I left there—I need those things. They're like lost swords in a fantasy book."

"In the meantime I'm supposed to be holding off the orcs?"

"I didn't ask you to be involved. I just asked for your legal opinion."

"In my legal opinion, you are a coward and quite possibly a nutcase."

"Then let's call it quits now."

"And what am I supposed to say when my morning visitor comes, 'Sorry, I've called it quits with John Reynman'?"

"That might be a very wise thing to say. I'm sure I'll be back before Halloween, they can shoot then. After that I'll be back for my mother's surgery."

"I am sorry your mother's sick, John—soon there will be no one left to take care of you."

Michelle hung up.

I haven't handled this well, John thought.

The balding man was chewing out his travel agent about some change in airline fares.

The next day Henry Crawford came to pick them up to

drive to Palo Duro Canyon. Henry drove a Ford Explorer, the same vehicle he had driven the night John had arrived. Mom had packed ham and cheese sandwiches, filled a thermos with iced tea, and had pretzels and other snacks for the forty-minute drive. Henry apologized for being late, and said he needed to get gas first.

John said, "Why don't you and I go get gas while Mom just rests."

Mom had no desire to "just rest" but John pushed the point and he and Henry set off.

"How long have you known my mother?" asked John.

"We met at Bible study last year, so I would say about nine months."

"How do you think she is doing?"

"Oh, you mean the health thing. It's hard for us folk to go to doctors you know. Each time we toddle in we're expecting that news that it's all over, the alarm bell is ringing."

"I wouldn't have thought of the alarm as a symbol for death."

"I didn't mean as a symbol of death. I meant it as waking up. You only really wake up if you know that your life is about done. I had a heart bypass a few years ago and I woke up."

"What did waking up do for you?"

"Well for one thing I bought a sports utility vehicle. But the main thing is, it taught me to have fun. Now fun is misunderstood. You ask most old coots like me what fun is and they'll tell you smoking cigars or drinking beer or some such shit. But fun is finding out what the hell has been hidden around you for years."

They had pulled into a place that gave a wash with a fill-up.

Henry said, "I love going through these places. Ever paid attention at a car wash? That's fun."

"Do you see a lot of Mom?"

"I think I know where you're headed with these questions, and I'll tell you now I don't believe in lying so don't ask any questions you're not ready to hear the answer for. You may want to stick with safe stuff like how many kids I have."

"So how many kids do you have?"

"Don't rightly know. I was a traveling salesman for many years. I sold safes. Small safes for stores. I thought briefly about becoming a safecracker when I had my bypass, for the fun of it, you see."

Great foam strips were smearing soapy water on the windshield; soon the big rotating brush would descend.

"Why," asked John, "didn't you go for it?"

"Well, there's the problem of getting shot, you see. Not a fun thing to get shot."

"Yeah," said John, "I know."

"You've been shot at? I thought you were a game designer. Competitive field, is it?"

"No, I wasn't shot at by a fellow game designer," said John, and suddenly he wondered why he had never considered his friends. The police always consider your friends first. John told Henry about being shot at in front of the Lost Weekend Pub without mentioning the double, or other related matters.

"The world," said Henry, "is a dangerous place. That's why it's good to move around a lot. Don't be a sitting target."

"You think you can just dodge death?"

They were pulling onto the street, water running down the sides of the vehicle.

"No," said Henry. "You can't dodge death, but you can occasionally dodge the little darts that death flings at you to soften you up. Running away won't get you much, but learn how to dodge, my boy, learn how to dodge."

"I'm dodging as best I can," said John.

"Did you know that Pantex has had some contamination problems?"

"No."

"Yeah, they were dismantling some B-61 bomb, it was the best-seller of the 1970s, and as they say a 'small amount of low-level radiation' was released. We got the usual BS about how safe everything was and how they had bagged the problem. They had to put stuff in the paper because people had heard the radiation-leak alarms go off. Hard to dodge that stuff you can't see."

Mother was waiting with their lunch packed in a brown bag and John's laptop.

John moved into the back, and tried to make it look like he was taking notes. He worked on some overdue stuff for GASA's storytellers series, and tried to tune out Henry and Mom.

IDOL THREATS: The Story

    The small, desolate village of Hentrace was the last place you expected to find armed guards. These pitiful-looking men, armed with rusty swords and despairing looks, explain their wish to know if you carry "idols of false gods."

    "Years ago, ours was a prosperous but unhappy village. The headman, Mandragor, had made a deal with the powers of darkness. Every home was required to have an altar to the evil ones. Once a year we held a lottery to choose one man or woman to be sacrificed. And each year, on the morning after the killing, three coins—

gold, silver, and copper—appeared on each altar, a sign of Mandragor's bargain.

"One year the lot fell on Susareen, the village farrier. She was not one of our people and did not know of the lottery. When she heard her fate, she escaped with her young son, Lalor. In pursuit of her, we discovered that she had sabotaged the horses' shoes, so that they went lame.

"The next morning, no coins appeared. Worse, we discovered that every coin of copper, silver, and gold already in the village had disappeared overnight, each replaced with a tiny toadstool. For all that year, we could have no coin in our village, and famine and disaster befell us. The next year, we made the proper sacrifice, and prosperity returned.

"Many years later, Lalor returned—leading a group of brave Light warriors. They went from house to house, destroying the evil idols. Lalor dragged Mandragor into the square and denounced him for his evil ways. Then the Lightbringers burnt his bones, but not before he laid a curse on the town: that evil would return to trouble us. The Lightbringers remained for many months, eradicating the worship of the idols. Then they departed to free the rest of this land from its many evils.

"Yet we never regained our

prosperity. Slowly and surely,
plague and famine have returned.
Somewhere a last idol must remain.
We seek it so we may destroy it
and free ourselves from the evil."

IDOL THREATS: Gaming notes

HOOK: While traveling the
adventurers come to Hentrace.

SPEAKER

STORY

CLIMAX AND RESOLUTION
The idol is a statue to Lalor
in a public square.

WHAT THE STORY MEANS
Make some pious remark about
idealized war heroes here. People
never pay attention to their
environment, etc.

The canyon was a deep red cut in the earth dotted with the dark junipers whose wood gave it its name. Turkey buzzards rode the thermals of the canyon, but they appeared to be barely off the ground as you approached the canyon. Palo Duro Canyon's lower levels were laid down before the great lizards were a twinkling in Jehovah's eye. The Prairie Dog Town fork of the Red River, tiny and constant, has cut away the multicolored strata since the Jurassic. John's mother had a degree in geology; he had eaten this stuff from birth.

White sand lies in the creek beds, the canyon walls are oxblood red siltstone layered with snow white gypsum, the canyon walls (popularly called the "Spanish Skirts") are crumbly talus in yellow, rust, pastel olive, and pastel lavender. Local opals, bluish white and pretty but uncommercial; gypsum rosettes; nodules of hematite; fossils of horses, rhinos, and dinosaurs; geodes; and celestite are hidden here. Vuggy opaline chert, agate bands, petrified palm and pine. The bricklike walls act as a furnace—it's always twenty degrees (Fahrenheit) hotter at the floor of the canyon than at the rim. Floor to rim is 1,200 feet. Total canyon length is 120 miles.

Henry paid the two-dollar entrance fee and they began making their way down to the red warmth.

12 A Mysterious Manifesto

Water is precious in the Panhandle. Indians grew squash and tomatoes here. Colonel Charles Goodnight wintered his cattle. An oil prospecting company tried to lay a well among the soapberry near the creek. The bit shot into the air out of the derrick. The boom could be heard in Amarillo twenty-three miles to the north. A historical plaque testified to this with white letters and brown background.

Mr. Crawford drove the park road around the canyon and then stopped at the Sad Monkey Railroad. The Sad Monkey sold postcards and frozen custard, had a cactus garden and a miniature train that you could ride. John remarked that it had been his father's dream to run the little railroad before his death. Herman had thought it would be nice to tell the tourists the little spiel as the train rode through the cholla and creosote bushes. The train was named for a large dolomite boulder near the canyon rim that looked like a bowling ball. Some claimed to see the face of a sad monkey in the markings. John squinted very hard. Alas, it still appeared to be a bowling ball.

John wondered if he had done the wrong thing by mentioning Herman in front of Mom's current squeeze. Screw it, you're always doing the wrong thing in life, what counts is to recover gracefully.

John jumped out of the car and bought them tickets on the train. The train was on the other side of an eroded cliff face, beautiful with its layers of red, gold, purple, and finally a deep blood red shot through with glistening veins of white gypsum. John pulled his laptop out and typed while they waited. He promised Mom and Henry large cones of frozen custard at the end of the ride. They walked off to look at the cactus garden. John pulled the seashell scenario up, but relaxed into the memory of when he had brought his parents here. He had just got his license. The big test for drivers in Amarillo was to drive down the steeply sloping road into the canyon. Of course in Austin there were roads he used every week that were steeper than the park road. But it was his chance to show off. He had worked as a clerk in a men's clothing store and had bought them the frozen custard with his own money. It was his rite of passage to manhood. He assumed that having a car and a license and money was the gateway to the Land of Pussy. That had proved a miscalculation. He didn't have an intense sex life till Argentina.

Would his mother remember that he had brought Dad and her here? Would she take it as a quiet sign of his approval of her life with Crawford, whatever it was? He hoped like hell she would, because that would save him from having to tell her. Gesture is easier than speech, sometimes.

Two couples with children had come along and bought tickets as well.

He turned off his laptop and put it back in his backpack. He didn't like people staring over his shoulder while he typed. He had never truly felt that designing games was a grown-up person's job, and he felt it even less when he was freelance. There was a certain weird shame in letting your postman see you every day. He suspected that half the neighborhood had some theory that explained his apparent lack of employment ranging from drugs to the CIA. Of course after the last few weeks, they probably all had theories about the matter.

The train came. He left his backpack on a picnic table and ran over to get in with Mom and Henry. Mom began fussing at him at once. He shouldn't leave that bag out there with his *computer* in it. Old instincts overtook him and he argued against Mom. No one would take it. It would be OK.

Actually, as the train jerked forward John realized what a stupid childish thing he had done. He was arguing with his mom about whether or not to take a jacket. He had descended through all the strata of geologic time and now he was fourteen years old again. He hoped like hell the laptop would be there when they got back.

The train set off past the Prairie Dog Town (population: two prairie dogs and one rattlesnake), continued past some fake Indian petroglyphs and around the bend from angle of arroyo to curve of creek, and came by a commodius vicus of recirculation back to the Sad Monkey station.

His laptop was out of the backpack; someone had written a letter on its glowing screen:

```
Dear Stanley Marsh 3,
    0. It has come to our attention
that the Secret Society Without a
Name, of which you may or may not
be a member, has claimed
responsibility for the Dynamite
Museum. Please be advised that
the Museum is actually the work of
the Brotherhood of Something or
Other, of which you may or may not
be a member.
```

1. BOSO has been active in the Panhandle region since the days Amarillo was named Oneida, and its first prank was erecting Lighthouse Rock in Palo Duro Canyon. We are still amazed that someone took us seriously.

2. The original road signs read Road Does Not Bend, indicating that all of BOSO were straight-arrow types.

3. The Triceratops Crossing signs are not pranks, but sober public service announcements.

4. BOSO has recently replaced the Amarillo Public Library (on 45th) with another building with exactly the same shape, design, and contents. The only difference is that the new building now contains a volume entitled *The Dynamite Museum Explained: A Guide to All Knowledge* by Thornton McCain.

5. If possible "Signs" will be replaced with "Sings." In this statement BOSO does show sympathy with the ideas of the Secret Society Without a Name. However, BOSO goes further by also opposing BBQ Pork Rinds not being counted as a vegetable on school lunch menus.

6. BOSO will continue its activities until its message "ROAD DOES NOT END" is properly decoded as "SEND A NOTED DOOR." When the famous door is determined (from other clues in our rebus), and delivered to the proper location (which is likewise decipherable),

```
we will return to our eternal
hidden home.
    7. Through its advanced
understanding of general
relativity, BOSO has placed
several signs in the future, where
they will appear at the proper
time.
    8. Re-Creation is Recreation!
    9. Age-old proverb says, "If
you let your cat set your Picasso
on fire, don't let your cat play
with matches!"

                    Sincerely,
                    Ye Grand High One of
                    Nothing in Particular
```

There was no one around the laptop.

"My heavens," said Mom. "What does it mean?"

"I bet we're supposed to take this letter to Stanley," said Henry, addressing the rich and famous by their given names.

John saved the file.

"Isn't that Lighthouse Rock?" began Mom.

"Yes," said John. "It's that eroded column that everybody tries to paint. Some people have done pretty well painting the canyon, like say Georgia O'Keeffe, but Lighthouse Rock has been the draw of the gross amateur. I bet there are as many paintings of it in Amarillo as Elvis on black velvet."

"Why would anyone leave us a message on your *computer*?" asked Mom.

"It isn't a message for us, it's a message for Stanley," said Henry.

"Why would anyone leave a message for Stanley Marsh 3 on my computer?" asked John.

"Why does he leave those weird road signs around the city?" asked Henry.

"He's an artist," said Mom.

That was an answer that covered a multitude of sins.

John said, "Let's get our ice cream and drive for a while."

They went to the end of the canyon, where a brave cavalry officer had killed a thousand horses to force a repentant Indian tribe to surrender and walk back to a reservation where sickness and starvation awaited to finish them off. They parked near the plaque commemorating the event, and walked to a picnic table. Turkey buzzards hovered in the blue air, their forms shimmering in the thermals. It was warm here, as warm as Austin—hard to believe that it was October. Bradbury country. The little manifesto on his laptop was a Bradbury thing, a minor mystery with a fun conclusion. Michelle was right, he had abandoned her and retreated to his past. He was going on picnics, having random fun stuff left on his computer by electric Luddites. Harry and Mom were speculating about the letter.

1. BOSO was real.

2. The letter was to them because Somebody knew that John and his mom had been at the twentieth anniversary of Cadillac Ranch, the biggest private sculpture in the U.S., belonging to Stanley Marsh 3; did you know the Cadillacs are planted in the ground at the same angle as the great pyramid of Cheops?

3. Someone wanted this to be part of John's game; you know you could make a nice game about those wacky road signs.

4. It was a message for Henry because he had voted for Nader (John had some trouble following this).

5. Perhaps if they left the laptop out and hid behind yonder

hillock, the secret sharer would appear to write something else.

6. Maybe you could get a novel or a game out of what was left behind like the shoemaker and the elves.

7. Maybe Mr. Marsh or the Dynamite Museum leave such messages on unprotected laptops. Maybe they're waiting in the bushes.

8. Maybe the girl that sells the ice cream did it.

9. Maybe they should check the Amarillo Public Library for a copy of *The Dynamite Museum Explained: A Guide to All Knowledge* by Thornton McCain.

At this point in the speculation John, having eaten his frozen custard, decided to climb the small hill near where they had parked. He needed to get away from this. Up through the gama grass he went, past juniper and thorny mesquite, his progress disturbing a meadowlark. It was an easy climb. At the top of the hillock a rough slab of greenish siltstone had been set on a block of rough beige sandstone. It looked vaguely like an altar. John thought that if this were one of his games, it would be a clue.

On the altar lay a shark's tooth.

John heard someone coming up the other side of the hill.

It was Cassilda, in a brown pantsuit and wearing a pith helmet. She cocked her right index finger at him, forming a pantomime gun.

"Bang!" she said. "I got you."

John stepped back suddenly, lost his footing on the loose red soil, and tumbled down the hill. Cassilda came running after.

"Oh my God! Are you OK?" she asked.

She helped him to stand up.

"What the hell are you doing here?" John asked.

"I live here—well not in the canyon, in Amarillo. You remember we were married."

"What are you doing here now?"

"Stalking you. Look, you go down to your folks and I'll get my tooth. It's good to see you, John."

"I think it's good. Did you say stalking me? Is this some kind of joke?"

"Look, you just fell and your worldview is shaken. That happens when we fall. Falling can be very magical. Don't damage yourself, walk down the hill slowly. Go sit with your folks. I'll be right down, I promise."

She turned him around to face the picnic table and gave him a little swat on the butt. He began walking toward the table.

"Hello Mom, hello Henry."

"Are you OK?" asked Mom. "You look like you've seen a ghost."

"Well I kind of have. I saw Cassilda."

"His ex-wife," Mom explained to Henry.

"Well that can be a scary thing."

Cassilda came romping down the hill and up to the picnic table.

"Hello, Elaine!" she said, and rushed to meet John's mother. "And I don't believe I know you?" Putting her hand out to Henry.

"Henry Crawford."

"Cassilda Jones."

"Cassilda, dear, what a surprise. I don't expect to run into working people on a Tuesday," said Mom.

"I work," said John.

"I know dear, but I mean real work—well you know what I mean."

"Oh," said Cassilda, "you might not classify me as real

work. I teach creative writing at the college and I tell fortunes at the Nine of Disks on Wednesday. On Tuesdays and Thursdays I have nothing to do so I like to come out here and write."

"Was it you?" asked Mom.

"Was it me what?" said Cassilda.

"That left that strange letter on John's answering machine, I mean computer?"

Cassilda denied this, and this led to John showing her the letter, and to listening to the speculation chain again.

"That," said Cassilda, "is very strange."

Henry suggested that they all go to the Goodnight Trading Post to get a soda. Cassilda asked if they would drive past her car, which was parked on the other side of the hillock, so that she could retrieve it.

At the trading post, amid the postcards of jackalopes and the cockleburs in acrylic paperweights (labeled "Porcupine Eggs"), Cassilda began to hum the theme song from the *Perry Mason* series. Every time John started to question her, she put her finger to her mouth for silence.

When it was time to go, Cassilda spoke up: "Oh John isn't going with you, didn't he tell you, we discussed this on the hill, he's going to drop by my house and we're going to catch up on some mutual friends."

"That's right," John said quickly.

"Well let me know when you're coming home," said Mom. "Give a call before you do."

Henry and Mom headed out, no doubt for a quick tryst.

John went to Cassilda's car, a huge maroon Buick land boat. It had belonged to her mother, John recalled.

As they began to drive out of the canyon, John asked, "You really did write that stuff on my computer, didn't you?"

"Of course. I had walked up to the Sad Monkey, and I heard you have your little childish argument with your mom, so I *knew* I had to do something to it. It really got you when you saw it open and up, didn't it?"

"Well, an OK joke. Joke because I was being dumb, but why did you tell Mom you didn't?"

"For the sake of Mystery. Mystery is a very rare commodity, you know. Didn't you see how she and her boyfriend came alive talking about it?"

13 Mason and Music

They drove on in silence while John was planning what questions to ask. They were nearing the city when John spoke up.

"Why the Brotherhood of Something or Other? Why BOSO?"

"Because we are all bozos on this bus. Aren't you going to compliment me?" she asked.

"For what?"

"For the clever way I got you here?"

"Picking me up in the canyon?"

"No, got you to come to Amarillo."

"Yeah," said John, "dumping a corpse in my living room sure got my attention."

"What?"

"There's nothing better than a dead man to cause a couple to get back together."

"What are you talking about?"

"Your messenger is dead."

"Mason's dead?"

Cassilda pulled the car into a quiet residential street, not far from where one of John's aunts lived.

"Not only dead, but he bled on our hardwood floor."

"What did he die of?"

"Well I'm not much of an expert, but I think it was the gunshot to the head."

"Tell me what happened!"

"No, my dear, you tell me, or perhaps you would rather tell the police."

"I," began Cassilda, uncertainly, "I didn't mean to, I didn't send him to. Oh my God, you didn't kill him, did you?"

"I don't think so, but I am unsure. There, I said it. I've been trying to say it for a while."

"Tell me."

"No! You will tell me first, tell me all. Think of how much the mystery of what I know will enliven you."

"OK, but not here. Where I work is not far, let's go there."

She got her car back on South Washington Boulevard and began driving north into the city. Stanley Marsh 3's "flower signs" were in front of many houses, a series of irises, daisies, petunias, poppies—a beautiful suite to remind the city that Georgia O'Keeffe once taught art in the public schools here. (She was fired because she didn't follow the textbooks, and then she went on to teach at the normal college in Canyon, Texas, and discovered the colors of Palo Duro Canyon, and the Mystery.)

After the flowers was another sign by Marsh, "If You Don't Like Art Signs Lubbock Is Due South."

As Cassilda neared the pleasant oasis of Amarillo College, she turned into the small parking lot of a small dark red brick building with large windows. Painted in the windows were the words "Nine of Disks," a smiling crescent moon, and some silver stars. Inside was a sweet smell composed of amber, sandalwood, and roses, trays of glittering crystals, jewelry, knives and bells, tarot decks and books on runelore, and a smiling old lady.

"Rosa," said Cassilda. "This is my ex-husband."

The old woman's grasp was firm, her eyes fiercely bright.

"I am Rosa Mackenzie."

"John Reynman."

John knew the name of Rosa Mackenzie. She had owned one of the larger ranches. Why would someone with beaucoup money be working in a little occult shop? It couldn't be a moneymaker here. Besides, she had to be older than God.

Rosa turned to Cassilda. "Well it worked out like you predicted, but I still disapprove of your method."

"You live for 'I told you so's' don't you?"

"It's one of the few pleasures for someone my age," said Rosa.

"We need to use your back room to talk."

"Well, certainly, but why here instead of your apartment?"

"This is something that I think needs neutral ground."

Cassilda headed for the door behind the counter.

It was a small friendly room painted rose beige, which Cassilda illuminated candle by candle. There was a slightly dilapidated table flanked by two chairs. On the ceiling was a zodiac mandala. The only out-of-place touch was a poster of the *Hindenburg* on the door behind them.

John and Cassilda sat.

Cassilda said, "I am normally here telling someone else's future, not my own past." And she began

THE STORY OF TAYLOR KEZIAH MASON

"I was going to live with my aunt when I moved back to Amarillo, but we made each other crazy. I got an apartment on

Amherst. In April, about the middle of the month, Taylor moved into the apartment across from mine. He watched me all the time. I thought it was because I'm good-looking. So I made a point to sun myself in one of my skimpiest outfits by the pool. He walked up and asked me if I was Cassilda Reynman. That was a shock—I took my maiden name back right after moving here six years ago. Nobody except your mom I think even knows your name. Yes, I said, yes I was. He said he had been thinking of doing a documentary on the Electric Luddites, and he knew that you had written a song for them, and asked if I knew anything about the band. Well I was close with their manager, as you might recall. But I hadn't seen Mary Denning in years and years. I asked how he happened to find me and he said he found me just by accident. He said he had come to Amarillo because the band's hometown, Becky's Ham, New Mexico, didn't have anything like a library. Later I realized that the band didn't come from Becky's Ham because I remembered Mary Denning's story about her finding out that the city was misnamed by a religious but illiterate pioneer thinking to honor the Messiah's birthplace. So I knew he was lying to me, and it was a lie he had researched to make to me.

"I still didn't believe him, but he said he had tracked me down because of an article in the *Amarillo Globe News.* We were interviewed and they did our picture. Remember? The band had left town and the reporter needed a picture, so somebody you knew in high school . . . anyway, we did have our picture made, and this guy says he had come across it. He went on to say he was doing a story on the whole early-eighties garage band movement, but the Luddites had a particular fascination for him.

"He also said I was very pretty and that I looked the same (or even better) than I had thirteen years ago.

"I thanked him, and we talked and he asked me out. So we

dated a couple of times. I mentioned to him how much he looked like you except for his brown hair, and he told me he was thinking of having it dyed blond. That really made me aware of how much I missed you on a physical level, so I encouraged him to get his hair dyed, it might change his luck.

"We wound up in bed the day after the dye job. He was good, but during the afterglow, I got to thinking. Here this guy was supposed to be researching a totally nothing band, and he had been in town for a month, with no apparent income. So I got up and put on *The Way Out*, Sally was singing 'Mirror Men from Mars' and he didn't do anything. No comments on the music, or anything. This man had just been inside me and here I was almost naked in front of him and he starts asking about any birthmarks you might have had. I ask him if he likes the music. 'It's OK,' he says.

"So I knew the whole Electric Luddite thing is a lie, and I'm pretty scared (and maybe a little turned on), and I snuggle up to him and give him a blow job, which as you no doubt recall I am very good at—you can trust a man when you've got teeth on each side of his dick. It took a little while, and afterward while he lay there quivering like jelly I asked him to talk about himself. He said that he hadn't always been a filmmaker, that he had been a mathematician. He came from a long line of scientists, he said. Keziah Mason had been a mathematician in Salem in the seventeenth century, and her great-great-grandson, Monck Mason, had set a transatlantic speed record for balloon flight. So I asked him if I should start the album again.

"He said he didn't care and then I grabbed his dick real hard with my right hand and I picked up that letter opener that you gave me—you know, the one with the ivory rhinoceros on it—and I pressed its sharp end against his glans. I said that I was surprised that he didn't care about the album, I thought the Electric Luddites were his favorite band. Just who was he and what the goddamn fucking hell was going on? He told me that he wasn't interested in the Electric Luddites, he was interested in you.

"OK I said, first how do you have enough money to spend months trying to screw John's ex-wife and second why are you interested in John?

"He said that money was no problem in his life. He had invented a data compression algorithm that had become the industry standard. Since he had a great deal of money, he had decided to devote his life to travel. He was going to visit the larger cities of the United States in alphabetical order. Anchorage had been cold as hell, Atlanta was too warm, Austin was perfect for February. He had stopped in a bar called the Lost Weekend. It was badly lit and done up for Valentine's Day, and this woman came over to him and started coming on very strong to him. She actually let him put his hand up her skirt and onto her bare quim. Well he had heard Texans are friendly, but this was a bit surprising. Then a waiter lit the candle at their little table and she freaked out. She had thought it was you. She apologized and was about to run away in shame, but Taylor calmed her down. She said her name was Clarissa.

"Taylor was fascinated by the similarity of appearance. He had had a twin who died at birth. 'All my life,' he told me, 'I've been looking for my dead twin. I felt that I wouldn't be whole unless I found some kind of brotherly dyad to be part of. Here was my big chance.' He got her to tell him everything she knew about you.

" 'I decided to research John Reynman then. I was going to remake myself to be as like him as possible. When I was perfect I would approach him, I would be a walking mirror of him.'

"Taylor began by researching your roots. He went to live in Lubbock in the same student ghetto you had lived in when you went to Texas Tech. He met with some of your old professors, under various pretexts. He came up to Amarillo. He spent an afternoon with your mom under the guise of an architecture historian. Did you know the house you grew up in was designed by one of the pupils of Frank Lloyd Wright? It's true. I bet Taylor knows—eh, knew a lot more about your life than you do. Elaine had mentioned me, and he moved into my apartment complex. He figured that I would be the biggest help of all.

"At this point I released his penis. I told him that I didn't believe any of it. He said he could show me, so we got dressed and went back to his apartment."

"He had a huge trunk filled with things connected with you. He would pull each one out and describe it lovingly like a stamp collector describing lot 49. He had a souvenir cup from the Fisherman's Luck; he had your report cards from kindergarten—by the way, I apologize for all those years you told me that you went to 'Snodgrass Hall'—I always thought that was a joke; he had this poem you had written in second grade about a visit to the zoo—it had a cute little rhyme of 'beige' and 'cage'—'beige,' that had to be a word that Elaine gave you; he had pictures of your dad, lots of pictures of you and of your brothers; he had a note your junior high Latin teacher had written to you in Latin; he had copies of all your games—both electronic and paper; he had a copy of *Dragon* magazine with that monster you and I wrote up; he had menus from your favorite restaurants in Austin; he had a picture of you and me from the Buckhorn Hall of Horns in San Antonio; he had your copy with your bookplate of that Rex Hull novel about Austin you like so well, *Night Music*; he had pictures of our house—I mean your house back in Austin; he had pictures of Clarissa—she's very cute by the way—do you only date women whose names sound like mine? Don't answer that, I want to fantasize that you do; he had a button from a shirt that I gave you.

"By the time he was finished with his show, I knew one thing. I knew that I loved you more than anything. I loved you as much that night as I did that dawn on the beach after we had buried the shark. I asked him what he was going to do and what he wanted from me.

"He said that when he was a perfect copy he would approach you, and the natural resonance between you would lead to a great friendship and eventually to brotherhood and beyond. He said that he would enrich you beyond anything you could do for yourself, and that the two of you would travel the world together. From Albania to Zaire. He would pay me for all the data I could give him.

"I knew this was my big chance. I told him I could tell him everything, but that it would be a week before I could see him—that I had to have time to remember and put my thoughts in order, then I would tell him. I told him I didn't want any pay except for his company.

"Here was a man that wanted to be molded, to be shaped. I thought I would remake him into the very image of what I wanted. If alchemists can make gold out of inert lead, what could I make out of that semidivine substance, human flesh? I began by making a list of all the good times we had and all the good things we did. I wrote about our trip to Bavaria to visit mad Ludwig's castles, I wrote about you sodomizing me at the San Antonio botanical gardens, I wrote about swimming in the moonlight at Crystal Beach, I wrote about watching the bats fly out of the Congress Avenue bridge, I wrote about the champagne balloon ride that we bought by contributing a couple of hundred bucks to public television.

"Then I made a list of all the things I wanted to do but you were too timid. I wrote about how we made love to Mary Denning after the concert, I wrote about taking up spelunking and discovering hidden caves in the Texas hill country, I wrote about opening a little bookstore, I wrote about visiting the pyramids of Mexico and cities of the Inca empire, I wrote about you taking up painting, and us writing short stories together. I wrote about going to the map room of UT and spinning the globe and putting my finger on it to choose our vacation in Indonesia. I wrote about taking the hot-coal-walking seminar with you.

"Then I wrote all the adjectives that described your good qualities—handsome, caring, loyal, creative, smart. Then I wrote all the adjectives that I *wished* applied to you—passionate, daring, energetic.

"Then I created a novel about you. It was a three-day novel, *A Golden Mirror for John Reynman.* I modeled it a little bit after Rex Hull's *Little Gardens of Happiness.* You know, one of his Austin novels. I blamed me for our marriage's failure. I took each one of the qualities that I didn't like about you and I assigned them to me, but I made it very plain that I had conquered all these bad traits. As a novel, it wasn't too bad. I culled a section of it and sold it as a short story to an anthology, *A Curious Volume of Forgotten Lore.* I took another part to my creative-writing class as an example of how to write. So you see, you're famous. I had him go over each section slowly and carefully. He grew more like my dream man every day. But he didn't fall in love with me. All he would do is look over the book and say things about no wonder you were the chosen one.

"I, however, fell completely in love with you through the art of memory.

"Every day I would teach him how to walk, to talk, to fuck, to watch TV. He taught me a great deal too. He was really into topology and fractals and all maths that deal with similarity.

His thesis proved that symmetry in physical laws can generate an infinite variety of asymmetries, and that these asymmetrical functions are in turn connected through the symmetry. This explains why physical laws are so beautiful in principle, so chaotic in manifestation. I can see this is not where you want this conversation to go.

"He kept asking me, 'Am I ready yet? Am I perfect yet?' Finally I told him that he was ready except for a last group of finishing touches. I would give those to him, on a certain condition. He said anything. I told him that he couldn't tell you anything about me. He protested that he didn't want to come to his new brother in bad faith. I asked him if screwing his brother's wife was an act of good faith. 'Ex-wife,' he said. I told him I would only give him the final polishing if he would agree to my conditions, so he agreed.

"I told him everything else I knew, how you ate an ice-cream cone, your guilty pleasures in reading, the tiny mole on your upper left leg, your fondness for gumbo, your habit of sneezing in the spring sunshine. Everything. Things that only I could know. Because I knew when he found you, you would have to come to me. You would be curious and you would come, and I would win you back—because you would be a different man because of the power of Mystery.

"I told all this to Mrs. Mackenzie, but she doubted it from the start. She said that she didn't think the universe could deal with two such similar beings. It would spit one of them out like a watermelon seed."

14 The Dice Box, Perhaps

Mrs. Rosa Mackenzie had brewed hibiscus-mint tea. It was a lovely rose in color, and great with ice and plenty of sugar. John helped himself to a third glassful. Cassilda was powdering her nose.

"This hasn't worked out very well," Mrs. Mackenzie said.

"Which?" John said. "Cassilda's getting me here or my being a murder suspect?"

"The latter would seem to be more of a problem. It wouldn't be the first time I've had suspicious people in my shop. Divination appeals to people at the margins. Why would anyone with the safe blankets of the bell curve keeping them asleep want to be awakened by dice rolling?"

"You remind me of a man I know, Dr. David Niles."

"Is he somebody famous?"

John had hoped that she would know him, that he could find the trace of some occult conspiracy shaping his life. There had to be a reason that he was here and his seeming free will seemed a damn poor one at the moment.

John said, "He is part of the Brotherhood of Travelers."

"That's an insurance company, isn't it? No, I can tell that's the wrong answer, it's in your eyes."

"I was just hoping you knew something."

"I know nothing."

"You know enough to keep this shop going."

"The toughest aspect of keeping this shop going is doing my taxes, my Social Security, and so forth. Dealing with archetypes is much easier than the tax code. Do you know how long the tax code is in comparison to the Bible?"

"I know it's longer."

"It's seven times as long. I heard that on Paul Harvey."

"So what do you do with archetypes?"

Mrs. Mackenzie said, "The tarot tells a story—not just as most people think, the universal tale of cyclic dynamism of manifestation, being, dismanifestation, remanifestation; but it tells a personal story of the deck designer—in the art, in the mathematical form, in the names for the trumps and suites. I am trying to design a deck to carry my essence on in the world. Don't you think that parts of yourself live in the games you design?"

"Sure," said John, "I could see that. Parts of my better self that doesn't make mistakes, that always wins in the end, that gets the girl and the gold."

Cassilda came in. She said, "Now that you've heard everything, let's go out and eat, unless you're too mad."

"I'm not mad. I may be mad when I get what you've told me all sorted out. I'm sort of flattered and I'm sort of in love I guess and I am scared and I'm skeptical," said John.

"And they say that men can't talk about their feelings," said Mrs. Mackenzie.

"Sure," said John. "I'm ready."

It was dark outside, that dark that fills the fall and excites children with the notion of the coming of Halloween. John was glad to be driven to a little burger place in the historical district. Route 66 had passed through Amarillo, it was 6 there. Now it was the place of junktique shops and re-created diners. There were antiques on the wall from the Great Depression, and men and women in their seventies and eighties who were listening to Tommy Dorsey on the CD jukebox. There were unhappy and happy grandkids running around and there were young couples from the neighborhood whose clothes told John that having the huge chocolate milkshake at the end of the meal was as much a treat for them as it had been for their parents' parents during the Great Depression. John and Cassilda ordered Sixth Street Specials—burgers served in a tortilla with salsa. Salsa had never been a part of historic Sixth Street, but the past changes with the times.

"So?" asked Cassilda. "Other than dead men in your living room, how have you been keeping yourself?"

"My fortunes have followed the gaming field. I'm pretty much out of paper games now and doing electronic stuff. As long as they need people who type, I guess I'm OK. I've almost got the house paid off."

"Ever put in that garden at the back?"

"No. I found that list the other day of things we were going to do with the place, and I haven't checked any of them off since we broke up."

"That makes me happy in a weird sort of way. I'm glad that all those times that I've visualized you I was looking at the right picture. If you had painted a wall blue or a ceiling red I wouldn't have had a good enough take on you."

"And you, other than trying to get me up here so that I would fall in love with you, how are you doing?"

"The creative-writing classes are fun, but I'll probably lose them. I tell the students too much truth about how hard it is to get published, how hard it is to write, how hard it is to not write. What they want to hear is how to be the next Stephen King. If I knew that, I wouldn't be teaching creative writing at a community college."

"What about the tarot stuff?"

"I like to rattle people's cages in what I hope are good ways. I like to shake people up so I don't tell them the usual 'You will meet a tall Mediterranean man' bullshit. I tell them, 'The spirits want you to do volunteer work cheering up old people in a rest home.' Or 'The spirits want you to put a bird-bath in your front yard.' Good for the old people and the birds I think and maybe it will give them a little self-knowledge while they do it."

"You think self-knowledge is a perfect good?"

"No. Not always. Sometimes it's a hell of a drag, but that's what people come to an oracle for. A little self-knowledge at a crucial moment when everything is in flux, and you've got a weight for your lever. If you know what you've made yourself to be, then you have a little anchor that you can move the world with. Even if things are stacked against you."

"What self-knowledge do you have?"

"It's hard for us oracles to have any self-knowledge; fortunately, Mr. Mason forced some upon me. I know that I want you. I still want to change you. But I want you more than I want to change you."

"I think I want you too, and I certainly think I want to be changed. Even with the bullets flying by I feel much more alive now than I used to. I think I see a little bit of what you've been trying to tell me over the years."

"Then you'll come back here, or I'll come to Austin?"

"No, not while things are deadly. Excitement I can share, but not danger."

"What if I'm willing to share in danger? That's what love is, you know, a willingness to share in danger."

"Well 'love' is a pretty dangerous word for people that have been apart as long as we have."

"What about lust?"

"Oh that's a much less dangerous word."

There was peach cobbler for dessert.

He couldn't keep his hands off her on the drive to her apartment. Inside she lit three red candles and some Russian amber incense, and then she went to change into a frilly little sea-green negligee that showed off her long legs and creamy breasts. She took his hands and placed them on her breasts.

"I've wanted this ever since I saw him," she said.

He began teasing her nipples, which were already stiff with desire; she leaned forward and kissed him, at first gently, but with a growing fever as his hands began to knead and pinch. Her kisses mainly landed on his mouth, but his ears and neck were not neglected. She moaned and with her right hand began to feel his hardness through his pants.

She pulled away and moved to her cheap brown sofa, an artifact of their marriage. She piled the cushions one atop the other and sat on them, pulling up the negligee and spreading her legs to show him another dessert. He dropped to his knees. He ran his hands inside of her thighs and pushed them even more open. He leaned forward smelling her musk, and began licking ever so lightly. He used long slow lashings of his tongue from her anus upward to the top of her vagina. She squirmed trying to get his tongue to spend more time on the clitoral hood, but he was slow and determined. He put his index finger inside her, very slow, very, very firm. Back and forth. Then his index and middle fingers. His tongue now spent its efforts on her clitoral hood, and as her vagina blushed with the violet of great excitement he began to suck on clitoris and hood. She thrashed about as she came, and she came loudly.

Three of her orgasms later he stood up, his face smeared with her juices.

He began taking off his pants. They had done this a thousand times before. She stood up and he took her place on the cushions. His dick was harder than advanced calculus.

She knelt before him. She began by washing his balls with her tongue while gently jacking him off. She looked up at him sweetly.

"Have you missed me?" she asked.

"I didn't know how much."

"Come on, tell me how much."

"More than I would miss reading."

She bit him very gently on the balls, then began licking the length. She continued till a little gasp escaped from his mouth, then she put her mouth on his glans. She sucked with an admirable greed while she tickled his balls with the fingers of both hands. She broke off after a while and said, "More than reading, huh?" He was beyond speech at this point. She continued, and a minute later he shot off in her mouth in three great spasms. He completely relaxed for the first time since he had seen the corpse, and while relaxing, shifted to the side and fell off the cushions onto the couch and the floor. They laughed for a good long time, then Cassilda went to her kitchenette. She returned with a bottle of champagne. Pop!

"To discovery!" she said, and they toasted.

"To travel!" he said, and they toasted.

"To more sex!" she said, and poured champagne on her breasts, where he began to lick and suck it off, chewing her bright pink aureoles. Her breath was fast now.

"Forty-three," she said.

It was the secret number of their honeymoon, when he had brought her off forty-three times (with some help from modern technology).

"Eleven." Proof of man's fundamental weakness in comparison to women.

She began fingering herself, he began chewing harder. He was getting stiff again.

Cassilda pushed him away. "Bed."

He followed her into her small apartment bedroom. The bed had a worn-out quilt on it, a gift from his mother when he had gone off to college—he wondered how it had got here.

She pushed all of the bed's clothing away. She knelt upon the bed. Her preference for doggy style hadn't changed over the years.

Nor had her wet tightness.

The games in bed continued late into the night; although played before, they had not lost their charm. Of all the games John had spent his life on, these were the most worthwhile—each in its moment of shuddering red intensity re-creating himself.

After she said twenty-four, there was just warm quiet snuggling. For a long time they had the silence that only true love can bring. Then Cassilda said, "Did you ever read the novels of Carlos Castaneda?"

"When they were coming out. You had them around the house."

"Did you keep them?"

"No. I sold them to Matthew."

"That's a pity. I think you should reread them about *dreaming.*"

"Why?" asked John.

"Well, in one of them, I forget which one, Don Genaro explains that his power as a *dreamer* comes from a dream in which he saw himself asleep. Once this had happened, his powers of imagination were stronger than the laws of space and time."

"You're suggesting that I have special powers since I saw myself dead."

"Well at some level you're bound to. Part of your soul must be aware of its deathlessness; that could be turned into power with the right experiments."

There was another silence—while John looked at the pot that was his soul and found it not yet boiling. He felt sticky and sore, so he got up to shower.

The nice thing about apartments is that you can shower for a really long time and not use up the hot water.

John washed and washed and washed everything away.

He was feeling a new man when Cassilda stepped into the bathroom.

"I think you need to go over to your mother's," she said. "Some woman named Michelle Galen is over there and she's in trouble."

15 Escape, a Move in Martian Chess

John's knees were weak from fucking Cassilda as he and Cassilda walked into his mother's house. Michelle cried on the orange crushed velvet sofa while Henry Crawford was trying to distract her with tales of Amarillo city ordinances.

"There's still a law on the books requiring every citizen to maintain a hitching post in the front yard."

Michelle looked at him and said, "Do you maintain a hitching post?"

"No."

"Well you should give me some money because then I would be your lawyer and that information would be protected by the client-lawyer relationship." She sounded serious.

As John and Cassilda walked into the living room, John's mother ran up to him in the dark and whispered, "She's in a bad way."

John was trying to piece together a few things. It had been—two, three days since he had spoken with her? He was also trying to figure out how to get Cassilda to go home.

As he walked into the light, Michelle's face bloomed and

then withered as Cassilda walked in behind him. She hugged herself, and started crying again. John crossed over to her, taking a handkerchief from Henry's outstretched hand and offering it to the crying Michelle.

"Mom," John said, "why don't you make us a pitcher of lemonade? You might want to help her, Henry."

The older grown-ups departed the room.

"My God," John said. "What happened to you?"

"My life was ruined because I met you and fell in love with you," began Michelle.

Cassilda took a chair across the room. She turned off the lamp nearest her, leaving the only illuminated lamp in the room by John and Michelle.

"I am so sorry. I didn't think what my running away might do. I thought you would be safe, you knew so little and had done so little."

"Oh John, I don't blame you. I still love you. Who is that?" she said, pointing toward Cassilda.

"My wife. My ex-wife. The woman I used to be married to."

Michelle said, "Hi. You're very nice looking. Are you in love with John, too?"

Cassilda said, "I am in love with John in the sense I don't want to see him hurt or anyone he cares about being hurt."

"That's a nice answer," said Michelle, "but it's an answer you're giving me because I'm all torn up."

John said, "What happened to you?"

"It was right after you called me. I got a call from Dad's rest home that he was having a bad night, maybe they hinted it was his last night, so I raced over there. It was dark. I parked in the light. As I walked up to the building, someone hit me hard on the back of my head. I didn't go down at first, and I felt them hit me again. Then I fell.

"I came to and I was hurting really bad. I was in your bed

at your house. My arms were tied behind my back. The short Indian woman with the *bindu* was sitting in your den watching *Samurai Pizza Cats.* I tried to thrash my way off of your bed, but all I did was knock off that radio alarm clock your mother got you when you went off to college. She came in instantly.

" 'Do not struggle or I will have to hurt you,' she said. 'I am only wanting to know when Mr. John Reynman will be returning, where he is, and what he knows about the death of my husband, Taylor Keziah Mason. I think Mr. John Reynman is responsible, or Dr. David Niles, or Ms. Mary Denning. But I know Mr. John Reynman is the key because of my husband's obsession with him. For a year he has been gathering information on Mr. Reynman in some far-off Texas city, Lubbock I believe, so that he could take Mr. Reynman's place when the Great Change occurred. And you are the key to Mr. Reynman.'

" 'Sorry to tell you different, sister, but John skipped town and left me alone. You may as well let me go. As a lawyer, I must inform that you that the penalties for kidnapping are very severe.'

" 'There will be no penalty, as you know the police have put themselves as far as they can be from this case. I hacked into their logs for the day of the murder and there isn't even a trace that patrol cars came here.'

" 'Well like I say I can't help you, let me go, John isn't coming back to rescue me.'

" 'No, you are to Mr. John Reynman what I am to you. It is mathematics.'

"We went on with this sort of interchange until it was time for *Rosie.* She went back to your den and I lay in bed, really needing to go to the bathroom. I complained but she made me wait until after the show. I can't tell you how much my arms hurt. She had a gun, and she held it with one hand while she undid the ropes. I had to use the bathroom in front of her. I tried to get her to let me put my arms in front of myself, but no go. God, I thought I would die when she tied them back behind me, I thought they would snap like balsa wood. But the human body is very adaptable. Someone came to the house around six in the evening. They brought some Chinese-style steamed chicken, rice, and hot and sour soup. I heard her talking to him. A male American, the same voice that had contacted me about my father's problems. I had been worried about Dad until then—then I started worrying about who would take care of Dad with me gone, and of my daughter, and of you, goddamn you, and I thought of the people who would miss me which turned out to be a larger circle than I would have thought and those people who'll probably be glad I'm gone, which was a pretty small circle for a lawyer. Anyway, I didn't get to see the man, just hear him, although I think if I ever hear the voice again I could identify him. She ate her meal first, then she untied me so I could eat my cold chicken and rice. It was so damn good! Then she tied me up. I hate October because it gets dark so fast.

"Well I wasn't sleeping. She went back to the TV. It was during *Deep Space Nine* that I planned my escape. I would wait till late at night, say about four-thirty in the morning, then I would wake her up saying I had to go to the bathroom real bad. I figured that she would be sleepy and confused. I would be real slow about it, and if her attention ever wavered I would jump off the pot, grab her gun and throw it in the toilet, and try to overpower her. After all, she was tiny.

"It didn't quite work like that. We got to the throw-her-gun-in-the-toilet part, but I missed. She went down for the gun so I ran out of the bathroom. I was at the door when she shot at me, and out in the street screaming. This pickup happened by right then. And I thought I was saved, but the man inside was the drunkest human being I have ever seen. He didn't want to call the cops or stop. We careened down the street taking out the street sign there at the corner, and he headed off toward his house. He plowed up some bushes getting into his driveway and then he grabbed me. He seemed to think I was a woman that he had tried to pick up a few hours before.

"He was easy to get away from. All I got from him was the bump on my head, and this one on my jaw. In the process I wound up holding his wallet. I ran from his truck to Koenig. I was near the bus depot and saw that it was open so I was going to go there and call the police. Maybe the little woman was right and the police wouldn't give a damn, but it was a hypothesis I was willing to test.

"When I walked in, I saw a woman who was a dead ringer for my captor using the phone. It turned out not to be her, but I had edged over to the ticket counter in the meantime. The man in front of me was buying a ticket for Amarillo. Suddenly that sounded really good. I wasn't thinking of the twenty-hour bus ride, I was thinking of you. I was thinking of not having to call the police and trying to explain all this, I was thinking of not having to see her again. So I got a ticket. The bus rolled out with dawn and I could sleep with my arms in front of me.

"When we stopped at Waco, I called the Austin police and I told them that someone was in your house that wasn't supposed to be there, but that was about that. When I got to Amarillo I looked up your mother's name in the phone book. I got a cab and you weren't here."

At this point Henry and Elaine entered with the lemonade.

"John," said Elaine, "perhaps you need to tell me why you're really here."

"Well, the first thing we need to do," said Henry, "is to get this young lady and John out of here. Perhaps we should all leave. If these people are looking for John, this is not a hard place to look to find him."

"Where do you suggest we go?" said Elaine.

"I could put you all up. I've got a big place," said Henry.

"No, not me. I feel safe in my home. I know a lot of widows don't feel safe in their homes, but I feel safe here. When Herman first died, my friends told me that I wouldn't feel safe at night, but I do and I'm not giving that feeling up. Besides, I have things to tell John. I've been afraid that something like this would happen to him. But you should take Ms. Galen to safety," said Elaine.

"What about me?" asked Cassilda.

"You're his wife," said Elaine. "You should share his danger."

"Ex-wife," said John and Michelle at the same time.

"Well, this is very exciting," said Cassilda. "I would rather be where the excitement is."

"Well, we'll take care of sleeping arrangements later. I've got to figure out whether I want to involve any or all of you in this," said John.

"We're involved because we know you and love you," said Michelle.

"All right," said John. "Let me think."

The clock belonging to Elaine's great-grandmother that dated back to the Civil War struck midnight. Most of the people in the busy darkness of the neighborhood slept; others chased away their fears with laxatives, booze, or sleeping pills. Most enjoyed the ossification of their imaginative faculties that would have kept them from ever imagining the kind of situations and scenarios that were running through John's head. Most had no idea that the message on the nearest piece of sign art read, "Life is strange isn't it?" All John could think of was *The Chessmen of Mars* by Edgar Rice Burroughs. In Martian chess there is a move called "the escape," where the Princess can move fifteen squares in any direction or combination to avoid capture. John tried to remember if you got one or two escapes in a game, which suddenly seemed very important.

"OK," said John. "Here's what we need to do. I need to get back to Austin, go to the police first and then clean up my house second. Michelle can stay here, for a few days, if that's all right with Henry. Cassilda should go to some random place so that Mason's wife can't find her if indeed she has enough information to find her. Mom, you shouldn't be here for a while—maybe Henry can put you up."

They all spoke at once denying the reason for his plan or their willingness to be a part of it. Michelle wanted to go back to Austin with him. Elaine wanted to stay at home and she insisted that John at least spend the night. Cassilda and Henry suggested getting all the guns they had and making a drive back to Austin. So he tried again.

"What if I go to Austin first, then Michelle, then if you really want to, you can drive down next week."

Once again chaos and confusion. The clock struck one. They could hear a police siren in the distance and it made them quiet. So John hatched a third plan.

"Henry, why don't you take Michelle and Cassilda back to your house? I'll stay here with Mom and we'll talk. We'll all get together for breakfast tomorrow at the International House of Pancakes."

Cassilda helped Michelle stand.

"Come on honey, we'll get you cleaned up and most of a night's sleep in you. Mr. Crawford?"

"Henry, please. You can be on a first-name basis with people you are sharing highly dangerous semiparanormal situations with," said Henry.

"Henry," said Cassilda, "I'll go to my apartment and pick out some clothes for Michelle, she looks about my size, and then I'll be over."

Henry and Michelle left, then Cassilda.

"I've always loved the lingonberry pancakes at IHOP. What do you suppose a lingonberry is?" said Elaine.

"Mom, you didn't ask me to wait behind so that you could talk about lingonberries."

"No, dear, that's a side benefit. I wanted to talk to you about something that Herman said about his boys before he died. You seem to be the one he was talking about. When the war came we got married quickly, so that in case something happened to Herman we would have that. We didn't know where he was going to be shipped. He was in the Army Air Corps, so we guessed that he would go on a submarine spotting base either in Brazil or Australia. Now he couldn't write me which, but we did have a code. He would draw a bag of apples for Australia and a loaf of bread for Brazil. His first letter came back with a loaf of bread on it."

"I know all this pretty well, Mom, what's the point?"

"Brazil, Recife to be exact, was a pretty strange place. For example one morning he woke up and there was an anaconda passing through the barracks with its head already out the back and its tail not yet in the front of the building. Things happen there that don't happen here, where everything is tied down really well. There was a Jew in his unit that came from a family of jewelers in New York. This guy was always spending everything he could on silver. There were massive silver bracelets down there you could buy from the Indians. You've seen mine."

John nodded.

"Well he talked your father into buying them, saying they were so cheap. So Dad started hanging around with the Indians. He mentioned to them that he was part Chickasaw, and that when he was born that meant his name was put on tribal papers. And since he was a cook he smuggled them some sugar and salt. So they liked him pretty well, and I'm getting these big boxes of silver, which bought this house by the way."

"I had never heard about the silver," said John.

"Well there's a reason. One day these Indians introduced your father to a white man that lived among them. I hadn't heard his name for forty-five years till tonight—Dr. David Niles. He was a photographer. He liked your father, he liked the way he was setting up for his future with the silver. He liked that your father wasn't completely ripping off the Indians like everybody else, but above all he liked how the fates of Indians in Brazil were connected to the people in Amarillo because of Hitler's madness. He said watching the weird interconnectedness of the world was why he traveled.

"He told your father that he had what it took to be a Traveler. He said that if your father wanted, he could introduce him to a long and happy life of Traveling mentally and physically. Herman asked about the war. 'Oh the war is nothing, no matter what we profit.'

"Herman liked the idea of not spending the next few years slopping out mashed potatoes to sailors, but he thought about me—I was pregnant with the twins at the time. So he turned Dr. Niles down with regrets. Dr. Niles wished him a happy life. Herman saw him once in Chicago in the fifties. Now our marriage wasn't real good then, and your father asked Dr. Niles about being a Traveler, but Niles told him about a man that ran for the bus one day and stumbled and missed the bus and as the bus pulled away he saw a violet-eyed woman that gave him a long soulful stare, and how he went home that day and wrote in his journal that perhaps he had missed his one chance by stumbling. Your father told me that to hurt me at the time, and I cried for about a week and then I went into premature labor and I had you. Your father was wrapped up in guilt and me in anger for about five years after that. But when we finally let go of that anger and guilt our marriage became better than ever. I don't know any couple that was as happy as us, and then we wondered if Dr. Niles had given us a second chance, or we had given ourselves a second chance, or what. Then for many years Herman interpreted it as he was in the process of stumbling in his marriage and that Dr. Niles had stopped him from losing me. Then he thought that maybe telling me the parable was his stumble—if he hadn't spoken we wouldn't have had five years of hell.

"But when your father was dying he got to thinking about you, and he said that the first years of your life were pretty bleak—which is probably why you're so bookish—but that your later childhood was super because of our newfound happiness. He said that you were probably connected with Dr. Niles just as Brazilian silver mines are connected with our house. He said he figured you would have to interact with that man or someone like him. I told him that Dr. Niles would be long dead, and I figured that I would never hear that name. But tonight that woman mentioned him. I want to know what's going on. I was always intensely jealous of your father because he had the chance to interact with Dr. Niles, while I was away from the excitement. That's why I always took Cassilda's side in your arguments."

John said, "Well sit down. I will tell you all. For the first time since I was twelve I will tell you everything."

16 Bright Like the Sun

"What," asked Elaine Reynman, "exactly is a lingonberry?"

The five of them—John Reynman, Michelle Galen, Cassilda Jones, Henry Crawford, and Elaine Reynman—were enjoying their breakfasts at the International House of Pancakes. Orange juice and coffee were flowing freely and John was practically inhaling the warm blueberry compote on his blintzes. John had always loved IHOP. As a child IHOP used to have small shieldlike decorations with four small-denomination coins of other lands glued on them. John, a coin collector from age seven, used to scheme of methods of stealing the coins. There was no answer on the lingonberry question from their table, but a male voice from the next table provided one:

"A lingonberry is another name for a cowberry, an evergreen creeping shrub, *Vaccinium vitis-idaea*, otherwise known as a 'mountain cranberry.' It is related to the North American cranberry *Vaccinium macrocarpon* and the European cranberry *Vaccinium oxycoccos*, a beloved berry of Finland. Ah the taste of Helsinki—reindeer steaks and cranberry pies."

The pale man with strawberry blond hair who had uttered this horticulturally enlightening remark was known to John. He was Kyle Gilman, a fellow student of Tascosa High School who had graduated in John's class. They had been part of the "brains," the contrastive pair to the "jocks." Before he could stop himself he said, "Kyle?"

Kyle looked surprised. "John? John Reynman? Man you are looking good. You look better than when I saw you fourteen years ago."

Kyle got up from his table and walked to join them.

Kyle continued, "You look younger than you should. What's your secret, man? What have you been doing? Now you told me you were married when we met last, which of these lovely ladies is your wife?"

Kyle had never been outgoing in the past. John wondered if he had been saving it up for this awkward moment.

"I—eh," said John, "I was married to Cassilda here. She was a sophomore the year we graduated."

"You're one of the Jones girls, aren't you?" asked Kyle.

"Yes," said Cassilda.

"I dated your younger sister a bunch of years ago, when I moved back to town."

Kyle had gone off to MIT and got some degrees in pure math, then had come home to work at Pantex, the top secret facility that assembled nuclear devices. John had always remembered his description of a bomb as "bright like the sun."

"So Kyle," said John, "you still work at Pantex?"

"No, the end of the cold war hit us a little hard, so I opened a travel agency."

Henry Crawford said, "That sounds like nice work."

"It's important work when you live in a small city like Amarillo. People want to go, they want to see things. The benefit is that I get to see things too, very economically."

Kyle at this moment actually pulled up a chair and sat down.

"So," said Kyle, "you still in games?"

"Yes," said Elaine. "John is here to research a new game about Amarillo, to do with Pantex where they store the plutonium, and the helium plant where his grandfather worked and those weird signs Stanley Marsh 3 was putting up around the city, and it could all have a climax in Palo Duro Canyon. It's going to have a whole level about Oprah."

"That's right," said Henry. "He's buying us breakfast and picking our brains. I used to work at the helium plant. You know we have a monument dedicated to the discovery of helium, with a time capsule that won't be opened till 2968. That's pretty exciting if you ask me."

"And I know about climaxes," said Michelle.

Kyle was a tad nonplussed by the last remark.

"Yeah," said John. "This is a working breakfast."

"Well I won't take up too much of your time, I just wanted to thank John and tell him how good he looks," said Kyle.

"What did you want to thank me for?" asked John.

"Well it was for turning me on to science fiction. You were the one who introduced me to it, and it's kind of why I got into the travel business. I used to be real serious in school, my only interest was math, but you used to be reading Bradbury and Lovecraft and Clarke. And I picked it up from you. At first I thought fiction was a bad thing, you know a waste of time, but I began to see more and more it was like you wrote in the paper for Mrs. Rhodan's class. 'Humans are creatures of the imagination and their highest duty is to imagine themselves in other spaces, times, and bodies.' I thought that was profound. Way back in junior high and it helped me start imagining math, which led to me to some good things, and it helped me start my travel business because that really helps people imagine. I bet you didn't know that you have an effect on people, did you man?"

"No," said John. "You know that's one of the nicest things anyone has ever said about me."

"Yeah," said Kyle. "When I'm booking some couple for Barbados when the snow is being blown about ninety miles an hour by that Panhandle wind, I think of you. I think of Mrs. Rhodan, too—jeez, remember the Atomic Fireballs?"

"Mrs. Rhodan," said John, "used to keep a huge jar of hot cinnamon candy called Atomic Fireballs on her desk. She would eat the things, and let any student eat them that wanted to. There was a weird rumor going around that a kid had *died* of them the year before we were there."

Kyle stood and shook John's hand.

"Safe journey," he said, and then left to pay his bill.

"You know, dear," said Elaine. "You do look younger. I have been thinking of that ever since you showed up that morning."

"You look just like you did when we broke up, maybe better," said Cassilda. "That man was right."

"Maybe it's due to good living," said John. "Anyway, I have decided my plan for dealing with Austin."

"Let's discuss this in my Explorer," said Henry. "I think we know that the tables have ears."

"Especially for lingonberries," said Elaine.

They tipped well and went out to the Ford Explorer. Henry began to drive east into town, and John began to talk.

"What I'll do is fly into town today. I'll contact the police and we'll go out to my house and be sure that they've gone, then I'll call Michelle and you can return."

"That won't do at all," said Michelle, "and you know it. We've got to find who these people are and then either talk to them, scare them off, or get rid of them. Otherwise it will just be like it was for me in the bus stop when I saw that woman who looked like my abductor."

"Well, what should I do?" asked John.

"I don't think you can expect help from the police," said Henry, "after what you told us about the Men In Black. I think people are watching you from two or three different sides at once. Maybe you're important, maybe you're a pawn."

"It's not bad to be a pawn," said Cassilda. "Pawns can become queens, the most powerful piece."

"If they stay the distance," said John. "But how do I become a queen?"

"Well right now, their power over you is that they know what's going on, and you are clueless. Now you probably aren't going to figure out a great deal more than you already know, but maybe you can look like you know more than them. Maybe you can weird them out," said Cassilda.

"I know that the woman who captured Michelle doesn't know what's going on—and that she thinks that either I do, or that someone somewhere is interested in me. She may have the real story on Mason or can at least clarify the link between him and Dr. Niles."

"So we go after her first," said Cassilda.

"What do you mean 'we'?" asked John. "This isn't one of my games. Michelle has been shot, kidnapped, and roughed up. This isn't funny, and you've no part in it."

"I do have a part in it. I'm the one that fed Mason all the information, because of me your house is full of weirdos, your girlfriend has been through hell—I caused all this to happen to you because I loved you. Besides, I can improvise some odd situations fairly well."

By now they were driving through the historic neighborhood streets that date from the one economic boom Amarillo had, after the discovery of natural gas in 1918.

"All right you can come along, but no one else," said John.

"John, I don't think anyone has died and made you king," said Elaine. "Your struggles are your own, but when they attach themselves to the people you love, they are their struggles too. This is how real life is different than your games—it spills over the neat boundaries of your life. I didn't raise you to be all hat and no cattle."

John hated that tone. His mother had developed it during her years as a science teacher. Not much else for a woman with a degree in geology to do during her time, and then the four sons took that away from her as well.

"All right so who's coming along to help me fight the bad guys?" he sighed.

Everyone in the car put up their hand.

"You are all fools, you know. I love you, but you are fools," said John.

Henry was driving by the Art Center now; across from it was an art sign with a visual pun on it. A big blue dot. Blue period. One of the few Picasso jokes in public signage.

"Well if John and I go first we can do something to lure the Indian woman to talk to us. If that works then when Michelle comes we'll be ready for bigger targets," Cassilda said.

"We've driven around enough," said Henry. "We've got a plan. We need to let these kids pack up and go to the airport. I'll take you home first. John, call and arrange a couple of flights. I'll take Cassy here to her apartment. Michelle, you can stay in my daughter's room till you're ready to leave. Elaine, I think you should stay with me."

"OK Henry, that might be good. They might be able to track me, but I think you would be a little out of their scope," said Elaine.

Henry began driving toward Elaine's neighborhood.

They passed an art sign:

SIGN OF THE TIMES

"You know, dear," said Elaine, "it's sad you didn't get to put those signs in your game."

Henry said, "No, those signs *are* in his game."

17 Ryoho Tai: Lone Star Gaming

"**Do you think we** need to clean the place up?" asked Cassilda.

"It's a good idea," said John, "so we look like more of a going concern."

"Bill's a little short on cleaning supplies. I see nothing has changed in that department."

"I thought you used to like Bill."

"I love Bill, he's so Bill-like, but you always had to fight your way through his apartment with a machete."

John sat on a folding chair behind a Formica-topped counter that had been the check-in for Lone Star Gaming. Outside across the small warehouses and concealed by them traffic whizzed by on 183. It was loud at ten in the morning and would be loud for another twelve hours, which made the rental of the small warehouse cheap. The tiny window showed nothing but asphalt; inside, flickering fluorescents provided a sickly light. Cassilda sat on a molded chair with a bright orange cushion. Tables were folded up along the walls, covered thickly with dust; during times of tournament play they had been put out over the industrial green carpet. A couple of the doorless closets that lined the walls were still filled with games—the cheaper games that Bill hadn't bothered to take home, and probably wouldn't until his lease ran out at the beginning of November. The door to the rest room at the back of the miniwarehouse was open, you could see the toilet, which could use a good cleaning as well. They had been sitting by the phone since 8:00 this morning, since the bait had been set at about 3:00 yesterday afternoon. There had been no bites.

Cassilda said, "Why didn't this place make more of a go of it?"

"Well for one thing Bill wasn't familiar with *Magic: The Gathering*, so the most popular game in the world wasn't being played here. Secondly, he didn't provide any kind of Internet access, or even computer games of any kind. Third, it's a crappy location—you can't see the store from the street because of the other warehouses, so there would never be any foot traffic or impulse buying, so Bill had to shell out the shekels for ads all the time. That's hard to do when you believe so much in your dream, you're hoping for people to just come. What he hoped for was a place where people could come down, play games, meet each other. He saw the whole thing as his last-ditch effort to preserve socializing face-to-face. Bill thinks we're all going to be just surfing the Net in the next few years, and he thought it was important to make a stand. God knows he owns every kind of game in existence from *Tunnels and Trolls* to chess, so he thought it would be great. He never got much of a crowd here. He gave it up about a month ago. Jeez, a month ago is so long ago now."

"The stranger your life is the longer it seems to take to live through it," said Cassilda. "Come on, if this is supposed to be a study group, let's set up a table or two."

They did so and pulled over the portable blackboard from against the south wall.

John wrote on it:

THE WAY OUT JAMES M. CASSUTTO
STUDY GROUP

REQUIREMENTS: $23.00 FOR
HANDOUTS INCLUDING A XEROXED
COPY OF THE WAY OUT

MEETINGS: TUESDAY AND THURSDAY
NIGHTS TILL CHRISTMAS
7:00-9:00 P.M.

TOPICS:

DREAM ARCHITECTURE IN THE
WAY OUT

THE CONCEPT OF TRAVEL AS SALVATION

"SECOND SAILING" IN PLATO AND
CASSUTTO

TAOIST INFLUENCES IN CASSUTTO'S
THINKING

FANTASY AND SCIENCE FICTION AS
FORMS OF TRAVEL

CASSUTTO'S INFLUENCE IN

CONTEMPORARY MATH AND PHYSICS

DID CASSUTTO ANTICIPATE CHAOS
THEORY?.

"Do you think we've got it covered?" asked John.

"Well I'm figuring Mason's wife knows something about what Mason was interested in. It was probably she who took his car. Unless she's just going to sit at our house, the ad in the *Chronicle* will draw her out, or one of her flunkies."

"And if it doesn't?" asked John.

"Then when Henry arrives with the guns, maybe we should all pay her a visit."

"Tell me again why we're not letting the police handle this?"

"If what you told me about the three men is true, I doubt the police are going to be much help. Besides, it's like you said on the plane yesterday, you have to know what's going on. It isn't just a matter of physical safety for you anymore. When you found out about your dad, you knew you had to know. It's like discovering that you have had another middle name all your life and not knowing it."

"Yeah, I know. I didn't tell you but I left the motel early this morning while you were asleep."

"I knew you left, I was just pretending to be asleep. Where did you go?"

"I drove to Dr. Niles's house. I figured that I would roust him from bed and force some sort of confession from him. There were no curtains in his windows and there was a sign on the front lawn. Vivian Darkbloom Realty. He seems to have moved on."

"Oh John, you should have majored in English instead of history."

"What do you mean?"

"He's having a joke on you. Let me ask you this, how long have you lived in Austin?"

"Sixteen years. Seventeen come November."

"Do you ever remember Vivian Darkbloom Realty?"

"Well I don't really pay attention. We bought our house from Oliver and Sterling. But it is a little bit of a Gothic name I suppose. It had a big purple-black petunia on it like those signs Stanley put on South Washington."

"Vivian Darkbloom is an anagram of Vladimir Nabokov, one of the names Humbert Humbert used or was it the other guy in *Lolita*? Nabokov is known for writing about doubles. I remember writing a paper in college referring to *Lolita* as 'a drunken stroll through the mirror-maze.' "

"So he knows I'm after him?"

"I would imagine that he knows something."

For a while they busied themselves dusting and putting things right. Then they left for lunch, and returned with cleaning supplies.

Cassilda began, "I hate to bring this up, but have you ever considered the legend of the doppelgänger, you're supposed to die within a year."

"Well," said John scrubbing out the toilet, "that's supposed to be if you see a living version of yourself. I saw a dead one. Maybe that means I will be reborn this year."

The phone rang. Cassilda answered.

"Hello, Cassutto Study Group . . . Yes, on Tuesday and Thursday nights, but you should come by earlier to pick up your materials. . . . Lots of interest in modern maths, we think Cassutto with his 'law of similarities' was a precursor of modern chaos theory. . . . Kirsten Munchower, yes definitely, both *Computers, Pattern, Chaos, and Beauty* and *Pawn of Chaos*. . . . Yes an interest of ours for a long time too . . . Twenty-three dollars for the handouts . . . Oh you have a copy of *The Way Out*, then you'll only need to bring twelve. . . . Tonight would be good, then you'll be read up for next Tuesday. . . . Yes, how about seven-fifteen? Good, see you then. . . . The instructor's name? Taylor Keziah Mason. Bye."

"Well?" asked John.

"A man, a younger man I would guess. He was pretty struck when he heard Mason's name all right. It was hard to hear him, there was some kind of music playing in the background."

"You think he's the woman's helper?"

"Well he for sure knows something about Mason."

"I'll set up the forms and the chair. Bill will bring the van."

"You think it will be quiet enough?"

"Bill says this place is real quiet, scarcely ever disturbed by customers when it was a business. If the guy's too loud I can pistol-whip him."

"Based on your long history of pistol-whipping people."

"Hey that was an option in *Laughter in the Dark*, my first espionage text-based game. You could pistol-whip anybody. If I can do it by point and click, I can do it in real life no sweat."

For the next couple of hours while they cleaned Lone Star Gaming, John practiced his "pistol-whip" move with the bottle of spare cleaner he was using. Eventually he broke the top of it off on a table and Cassilda came running with towels to catch the spill.

They were too nervous to do much more than clean. They left for dinner about five-thirty. Worried that the place would be "cased" while they were gone, they were careful to leave the light on and place the blackboard so that it could be seen from the tiny windows.

They went to a chain steak house on 183. It was the kind of place that both of them hated, but they were too nervous to eat much. John asked about Cassilda's writing classes back in Amarillo.

"I tried to teach them that writing wasn't the road to quick money. I was hoping to get the idea across that writing was a lifestyle, so I had them read about Kamo no Chomei, a medieval Japanese poet. Chomei was the secretary of the poetry office of Emperor Toba II; he was one of the great compilers of the *Shinkokinshu,* one of the imperial anthologies. He worked hard in his office until a great fire destroyed Kyoto. He then chose to live as a hermit. He had some revelation in the great fire that destroyed the city. It was as if in the great tragedy a great artistic fire destroyed all that he had been, but let him burn anew with a new vision. He composed a great list of styles—one of his favorites was 'old words in new times.' Others included the *Rakki tai,* the style for mastering demons, or the *ryoho tai,* the style of the double in which an object and a style mirrored each other. Another was called *sabi,* which means 'rust' or 'solitude.' I told them if they wanted to write they had to look for that moment of catastrophic awakening that set them apart from the world. Then they should write about what they know, but not before, not while firmly cemented to the world."

"Pretty strong stuff for an adult extension course. How did they take it?"

"They would nod politely and ask me how to format a manuscript or if they needed to get an agent. I wanted to tell them that writing is all a discourse on memory. That good writing should aspire to the condition of poetry, which is the memory of language. But I doubt that I opened any doors."

"Why did you keep at it?"

"That's an old question from our marriage, I would keep at

it but you wouldn't. That's an unfair shot, it's clear that you're changing. I keep rolling my rock up the hill because it makes me happy. Perhaps somebody will be awake for two minutes while I talk and they'll catch on. That's all I can hope for."

"That's what I promised Dr. Niles, that I would wake up."

"Well I hope you're awake tonight. I don't want to have to spend much time alone with that guy."

"Never fear, Reynman is here."

Bill had arrived with the van when they returned. Night was coming to claim her own. It wouldn't do to have Bill's van too close to the entrance, so the "love machine" was parked in front of the entrance to an opposite miniwarehouse, a place that sold archery supplies during the day. The van's back windows were exactly the height of the warehouse's windows. John wished that Bill hadn't put a bumper sticker on the van that read MAKE OUT MACHINE, it didn't seem to speak to the gravity of the situation. Bill had been that way since his divorce. Cassilda went inside to wait. John watched while Bill got the duct tape ready.

Bill began his stories about the number of teenage girls he had drilled in the van. John had heard all of this before. If any teenage girl was so hard up for love that Bill appealed to her, John fervently hoped that he wouldn't have to see her in full daylight. Bill habitually wore shirts that were too small. He was the only man whose navel John saw on a regular basis.

Like all old gamers their talk shifted to FRP games they had had in their twenties. Bill was talking about this time they were after a group of lizard men, which they had trapped in these cliff dwellings, and they were able to use the very siege towers that the lizard men had previously constructed against them. Bill, like all old gamers, tended to forget that these exploits were not a sign of his cleverness in the real world, but merely what the dungeon master had allowed. They were in no way different from his tales of scoring with young things, so sweet and willing.

A car pulled into the parking lot. It could be Mason's car, but darkness made it impossible to tell. It circled around. Both Bill and John ducked, as if the driver could see through the van's high windows. It parked in front of Lone Star Gaming. It seemed to just park there for a long time.

After a while a man got out and walked in. John could see him clearly with the opera glasses that Bill had brought for the occasion. He was young, thin, with light brown hair, and looked familiar. He was engaged in an earnest talk with Cassilda. He kept looking around. All of the closets and the bathroom had been purposely left open. John wished he knew what the guy was saying. Then he recognized him. He was the waiter from the Lost Weekend Pub, the one to whom John had said his name was Thomas.

It didn't seem like he was going to sit down. The plan was that he would sit down in the molded chair away from the door. John got out Bill's gun. It was heavy and it felt greasy from the sweat in his palms. Bill was hanging a couple of rolls of duct tape from his jacket.

It was a cold night, which is rare in Austin. You couldn't see any stars, which is always true near the interstate.

It didn't look like he was going to sit down. Cassilda looked nervous. Maybe this guy was threatening her.

Then at last he sat down, and Cassilda handed him a pen and the forms, the quiz they had made up on *The Way Out*. He began answering the questions, and John erupted from the van. He ran as fast as he could, carrying the gun in his right hand. He threw open the door of the miniwarehouse, and he yelled, "Freeze, don't turn around, I'm not joking!" and then he fired the pistol, aiming across the room and into a graffiti sentence in the bathroom—*Who's afreud of the big bad dream?*

"Don't move! Don't even breathe!" yelled John.

Bill was in behind him, having covered his face in a ski mask. Bill was saying, "I am going to come up behind you real slow like and I'm going to tape you to the chair. If you resist, the man with the gun will end your miserable little life. Do you hear me, you little bastard?"

The line was from a sharecropped novel Bill had written for GASA.

"I'm not moving," said the man in the chair, "but you can't keep me, there are people who know where I am."

"That's what I'm counting on," said John. "And why we're going on a little trip."

John walked up to the man and held the gun to the man's head. Cassilda removed his car keys. Bill taped him to the chair.

John did pistol-whip the guy. It took four blows to render him unconscious. Bill and John carried him to the van while Cassilda set up the video camera behind the counter to record.

She drove off in the car the man had brought.

Bill, John, and their passenger drove off in the van.

18 Benefits of Birching

The Middle Fiskville Cemetery is named after the little fragment of Middle Fiskville Road that dead-ends into it. Middle Fiskville Road used to run long and straight due north from Austin. It had two sister roads, East Fiskville and West Fiskville, that are totally obliterated now. Middle Fiskville exists in two- and three-block chunks throughout the north part of the city. They had been the gateways to Mr. Fisk's dream community. He was going to build a new and better Austin in the twenties, a beautiful suburb where all the moneyed betterness of Austin would be reflected. Unfortunately, the Great Depression intervened, and the new town vanished, only to be eaten by Austin in the better years of the seventies. The cemetery alone remains, very quiet and suitable for interrogating people caught in out-of-business gaming saloons.

They had his name from his wallet. Vincent J. Brugsch. They had a card table set up in front of him. Bill had provided a small electric camp lantern, while Cassilda checked to see that the cedar trees hid the illumination from the possible passing car. The only people one was apt to meet here, she realized, were make-out-crazed teenagers.

She laid out a tarot reading in front of him. John and Bill remained behind him. Bill splashed some blue sports drink in his face. He came to. He was groggy and couldn't talk for a while. Then he started to let out a scream. John reminded him of the gun and cautioned him to be quiet. Bill started the tape recorder.

Cassilda began her spiel.

"This is you, the Knight of Cups; here is where you're from, the Hanged Man that was your part in the kidnapping of Michelle Galen; here is your hope, the Lovers—perhaps an indication of your interaction with Mrs. Mason; here is your fear, the Ten of Swords, you are wisely afraid of the forces behind your back that are willing to kill you; here is your future, the Thirteenth trump, Death, now that stands for a radical transformation. Either you tell us all about Mrs. Mason, which will radically transform you, or my maddened partners will prepare you to join those around us."

A little of the light from the tabletop spilled onto the guy's lap. John noticed that he had a hard-on.

"I'm not going to tell you anything about Mrs. Mason and me," said Vincent.

John motioned over the guy's back to his crotch. Cassilda noted the bulge, and slapped the guy full on the face.

"You will tell me you little worm, because you want to tell me. Little worms like you always want to tell Mama."

She absentmindedly caressed her right breast and then slapped him again. Bill, who suddenly figured out what was going on, chuckled.

"I say you will tell me, or maybe I'll just give your sweet ass to my associates," said Cassilda, and slapped him three times hard.

"No," he said.

"Yes," she said, and began pulling his hair.

"Yes," he said.

"Yes mistress," she said.

"Yes, mistress," he said, bowing his head in shame and excitement.

"From the first, you will tell all," she said.

"I meet Chandra months ago when she and Taylor were coming to the 'Cup of Grue' lectures at the Lost Weekend. They knew Niles and they seemed to know everything he was saying before he said it. They really wanted to suck up to him. After the lectures Taylor and Niles would go off and have a drink together. Bildad, Chandra, and I would drink coffee. Sometimes we talked about the lecture, sometimes about Austin politics or the weather or whatever. She was cold to me, I loved her. All I could think of was what it would be like to be birched by her."

Cassilda backhanded him. "But she is nothing compared to me, is she?"

"No, mistress."

"Go on."

"One night I began to talk about S&M a little bit with her, you know, jokes and stuff. Bildad doesn't like that sort of stuff at all, so he excused himself. She admitted that she had been a top back in India, that's where she met and married Taylor. He had been lecturing on some math topic in Bangalore, and they had mutual friends. No, he wasn't interested in her as a top, just as a woman. He needed a woman for certain magical experiments—some kind of remote viewing or something, I never quite got it. Anyway she loved him very much. He had taken her away from a bad family situation, and grinding poverty. Not poverty by Indian standards, but by the standards of the people she would meet at the university. She had been everywhere with him. He would glimpse things sometimes when they were making love and off they would go. She admitted that she missed being a dom, and I told her that she didn't have to look hard for a little slave boy."

Cassilda slapped again. "You're awfully uppity for a bottom."

"She looked me up a couple of weeks before Taylor was killed. She wanted to play. She didn't tell me much but I got the feeling that Taylor wasn't paying much attention to her and that she was running scared. That's how I know that you are a much better mistress, mistress, nothing would scare you. I mean just look at where we are."

She reached over and dug her nails into each of his nipples. "You're getting off topic," she said.

"Yes, mistress, sorry mistress. When Taylor turned up missing she told me that it was big news, that he had been working on some top secret math stuff for the government, stuff about parallel universes or parallel lives or something like that. She found some phone number that Taylor had, and made me call it. It was John Reynman Games. I was supposed to invite John to the Lost Weekend so we could get a look at him. He showed up there with that Michelle. He looked just like Taylor, or at least like Taylor looked after a long trip that he hadn't told Chandra about. Meanwhile she found out that Taylor had been killed. She's got some friend in the police force. She claimed the body, and had it cremated. She got a visit from the government and they told her that Taylor's death wouldn't be investigated. So she decided to investigate it. She found out where Reynman lived, and then found Taylor's car. She gave me the car. Can I have something to drink?"

"Maybe later, slave boy, if you make your mistress happy." Cassilda reached over and dragged her nails across the bulge.

Vincent looked as though he was about to swoon from

pleasure. "Reynman skipped town. She didn't know where he was. She didn't know if Reynman had killed Taylor or if they were on the same side, or at least had common enemies. But she did know that she was going to find her husband's killer and kill him or her. It's the reverse of that Indian custom of throwing yourself on your husband's pyre. She knew that Reynman loved Michelle—she had watched them together after she had taken a pot shot at Reynman and missed. So she knew if she got Michelle, she would eventually bag Reynman."

John started to speak, but realized that Cassilda had better keep calling the shots.

She asked him, "Did you help abduct Michelle?"

"Yeah, it was pretty easy. The night that Reynman was deafened, he and Bildad and Niles had a talk. I gave Michelle a couple of Patron margaritas to steady her mood and she told me her name and where she worked and that she had never been shot at and that led to her talking about her dad, who had been in World War II and had been shot at, and afterward it was just dreaming a scenario. Anyone into B&D or S&M is good at coming up with a scenario."

"But you didn't like kidnapping her, did you?" asked Cassilda, stroking his face in a compassionate gesture.

"No, ma'am."

"Why not?"

"I was jealous of her, ma'am. There she was getting all the attention. I was sleeping in the front room, and Chandra had forgotten about me. When the woman got away from Chandra, I kept Chandra from chasing her into the street. Chandra was vicious with me afterward."

He smiled.

"What did you do after Michelle got away?"

"We continued to live at Reynman's. Listening to his answering machine for clues. I've got a job, but Chandra seems to have a source of money, or maybe she just doesn't care. She saw the ad in the *Chronicle*, and she sent me to sign up for the Cassutto study group. When we got the car back, she saw that there were two books missing, so we had called around town and found a copy at Adventures in Crime and Space. It was back in their used science fiction room. Chandra said it was one of Taylor's favorite books; she spent hours poring over it. When she saw the ad, she figured it was either some kind of trap or a chance to meet people who could help her out. It might even be Taylor back from the dead—she had some theories that maybe he was trying to skip over into Reynman. She said she would be there in fifteen minutes after I went in, so I would be safe. She'll come after you."

"No," said Cassilda. "She won't because she doesn't care for a pathetic little worm like you. That's why she sent you out to meet us. She just hoped you could find out something. What have you discovered? The paths of glory lead but to the grave." Cassilda managed a Wicked Witch of the West laugh that would have been funny anywhere but here. She continued, "And you know what, worm boy, you're not going to run back to little Chandra, because you've never had it this good, have you?"

Cassilda stood up and took her blouse off. She took off her bra and stood with her breasts less than an inch away from Vincent's face.

"Tell me you've never had it this good," said Cassilda.

"I've never had it this good," said Vincent.

She brushed his eyes with her nipples.

"I am going to let you go, and you will go home and wait by the phone for the rest of your miserable little life hoping that I will call you."

"Yes, mistress."

"Now cut him loose. You are not to get up until after you hear our car drive away, because if you do, I will never, ever play with you again. Is that clear?"

"Yes, mistress."

Cassilda shut off the camp light. She took the death card from the table and put it in his front pocket. Bill reached from behind and held his hands over Vincent's eyes while John and Cassilda folded up the table.

Then Cassilda showed Vincent the keys.

"See these, worm boy? These are the keys to your car. You will need to get down on your hands and knees and crawl among the graves to find them after we're gone. Remember what I said about not leaving your chair until after you hear us drive away."

"Yes, mistress."

Bill took the big machete from the van and cut the duct tape.

They drove away.

John asked Cassilda, "You ever do that before?"

"An S&M scene in a graveyard at midnight for the purposes of interrogation? Yeah sure. Like who hasn't?"

Bill burst into laughter.

John said, "I suggest that we don't go back to the store for a few hours. Chandra is likely to be a shoot-first type. We'll pick up the video of her in the morning."

Cassilda said, "We can pick it up on the way to the airport to pick up Michelle."

Bill said, "What's our next step?"

"Well, *my* next step," said John, "is to find out who killed Mason and what Mason wanted from me. That has always been my second question after I saw the body. Why me? I need to get Chandra out of my house. Maybe I can just talk to her and convince her that this whole thing is as big a mystery to me as it is to her. I don't think we learned anything useful from worm boy."

"We learned a great deal. We learned that Chandra has a great obsession for Mason, we got his confession about the kidnapping—although, as I'm sure Ms. Galen will point out to us, not in a form that has evidentiary value—and we know she has a friend in the police department," said Cassilda.

"We also know that the government paid her a visit," said Bill. "You know the government must know that you didn't do it, or you would be long gone by now the way things sound."

"Not particularly," said Cassilda. "They were interested in what was in Mason's head. They probably don't hold a grudge. Besides, he was probably manipulating them."

"So where am I driving to?" asked Bill.

"Well we could just drive for a while, it's such a beautiful moonless night, a night this dark you have to love," said Cassilda.

"Why don't you drive to my home?" said John. "See if anyone is around."

"Yeah," said Cassilda. "One of you guys could take a dump in a paper bag and we could set fire to it and put it on the porch and then run off."

Bill and John laughed.

"Wait," said John, "you're serious, aren't you?"

"As cancer," she said. "If we're trying to disturb her mind, what would be more effective? Show her who she's dealing with."

They stopped at an Albertsons, went in and bought Mexican vanilla ice cream as well as lighter fluid and matches, and insisted on paper instead of plastic.

Bill felt he could provide the required substance so he went behind the store to perform his duty.

Success, ample success.

Cassilda drove. The boys in the back folded the top of the sack shut and squirted it with lighter fluid when Cassilda pulled into her old neighborhood.

"Oh John," she said. "You let my snapdragons die out, there's nothing in your flower beds. I need to come live with you again so that I can start up a garden."

The porch light was on at John's house. John's neighbor across the street was watching TV, no doubt haunted by the six words. All of the words started with S, John remembered as the van pulled to a stop three houses away in front of the house of the veteran who always displayed the flag on holidays. John sprinted down to his house. As he stepped in the cone of light, he realized that for all he knew Chandra was standing on the other side of the door ready to blow him and his sack of shit away. Well, so be it. Someone had played a little trick on him, it was time to play a little trick back.

He set the sack on the porch.

The first match wouldn't light, he was too nervous, nor the second. Then he took a deep breath, centered himself, and lit the third.

He touched the match to the bag and it caught.

He stood up and rang the bell three times and then he peeled out of there like there was no tomorrow. He had never done things like this when he was a kid. He was sickly and bookish. He ran through his neighbor's yard. God it felt good. He plunged into the back of the van, and Bill helped to pull him in.

He turned and saw a woman open the door very cautiously. It might have been his imagination, but he thought he saw a gun glittering in the light of the streetlamp and the small holocaust below.

She immediately began stamping out the fire and squishing shit on her shoes.

John yelled and Cassilda took the van out of there.

19 Two Horses

The intrepid heroes drove to a twenty-four-hour bakery and had fresh hot doughnuts. It was nearly three in the morning. They agreed that they should go pick up the video of Chandra Mason in Lone Star Gaming, but as their gaiety ran out, their need for sleep took over. They decided that they would pick up Michelle at the airport tomorrow and go get the video then. John felt very, very tired. He realized that his right big toe was beginning to swell and ache. His father had had gout and all his life he had expected it.

Bill took them back to Motel 6. Cassilda gave him a pain-killer that she had in her purse, and the next thing that John knew she was shaking him telling him it was time to get up. He couldn't remember lying down. He had slept in his pants. He smelled like a horse. He shaved. He showered. He got to the rental car. The toe really hurt. Cassilda drove.

"You look too bad to drive," she said.

"You know I need to talk to you about Michelle," he began.

"Yeah, you probably do, but not now, not on the way to pick her up because that will make things worse."

They stood in front of the gate. John had to sit down and take some weight off of his foot. This was bad: if they merely scared their enemies away, John would never find out *what* had happened to his father. Maybe the gout was kind of a spiritual message from Dad. *I'm here, son.* That would be typical for the old man. He always said pain was good because it made you do what you needed to in order to become healthy; Herman's big dream was to make stupidity painful.

Michelle came off the plane, beautiful and rested, exactly the opposite of when they had last seen her. She didn't seem overjoyed to see Cassilda, but ran to John with genuine concern. "My God, what's happened to you?"

"I'm a little under the weather."

"I tried to get him to stay at the motel," said Cassilda.

She had said no such thing, and John wondered at the lie.

"We'll get you a room there for a couple of days. You can visit your apartment but you probably don't want to stay there until we've had our little talk with Chandra Mason," said John.

"I want to talk to my daughter and to Dad, but we can start out with getting a room for me," said Michelle.

"We need to stop and get the video. Have you had breakfast?" asked Cassilda.

"No," said Michelle.

"Well we'll pick up the video and then we'll have breakfast and then we'll get you a room," said Cassilda. "Bill is supposed to meet us about noon so we can plan our encounter with Chandra."

As they drove to Lone Star Gaming, they told her about the night's events.

The lights were on at Lone Star Gaming. Someone had closed all the doors to the closets and the bathroom and erased the blackboard. In its place was written:

I KNOW WHO YOU ARE

"And I saw what you did," added Michelle. "That was a great movie. We're such city dwellers that our biggest fear is that somebody knows who we are, or where we live."

Cassilda removed the video camera.

"It shot the full cassette," said Cassilda. "We have that, the taped confession, and Michelle to identify her if we want to go the legal route."

"As much as she deserves punishment, I would rather have the whole story. God I'm beat," said John. He plopped into one of the slightly rusted folding chairs and folded his arms on the counter and closed his eyes.

"Not just yet, lover," said Cassilda. "We've got to get this little lady fed and roomed."

"Yeah," John said, not raising his head.

"You don't have to take me to breakfast, I'll call a cab," said Michelle.

"Why don't I take you to breakfast," said Cassilda. "And we can finish that talk we began at Henry's. John, I'll take you back to the motel."

"Just leave me here. I can sleep for half an hour, then I'll be fine, really. I think that painkiller is making me drowsy."

"Are you sure?" asked both women at once.

"Sure."

"Well then," said Cassilda, "we're out of here. After I have Michelle planted at the Motel 6, I'll come back for you."

John was asleep by the words "Motel 6."

He did not hear the door close as they left. He did not hear the bathroom door open five minutes later. He didn't even respond to the .22 that nuzzled his ear, but the slap woke him.

"Tired after your night of high school pranks?" asked Chandra Mason. She was wearing a charcoal gray woman's business suit. Her accent was a great deal less than John had expected. She was carrying a small pistol. "It is an amazing likeness, you know. He so wanted it to be perfect. He wanted you to be named Dixon, you know. After Jeremiah Dixon (1733–1779), the surveyor who worked with the astronomer Charles Mason. Perhaps we can arrange to have that name given to you posthumously."

"We don't have to fight, Mrs. Mason, I don't hold anything against you. Where did you come from?"

"After your prank last night, I decided to meet you, so I came back here and hid in the bathroom. You came with your women, so I hid. But I have answered enough of your questions."

"If you hid, you heard. We've got enough stuff on you for the kidnapping charge, and charges for your shooting earlier."

"That isn't of much interest to me. All I want to do is revenge my husband. Have you heard of suttee? The practice, long since forbidden, of a woman following her man to the funeral pyre? I don't care if I live or die in my quest. I just want to be a *sati*, a virtuous wife. It is a form of the word 'existing,' *sat*. All of my existence is my love for Taylor Keziah Mason."

"I didn't kill your husband. I don't know why your husband was in my house."

"But you are the root cause of his death. Why did he waste so much time and money to have himself remolded as you? You must know."

"I have no idea. I want to know. Let's you and I work together on this. We have a common problem."

"What problem would that be?"

"The problem of a needful curiosity. We have both got to know."

"I am unsure if that is really my problem. I just want to revenge a good death to balance everything out. If I cannot find the correct target, you will do—you will do even if I don't find out. You might even do better."

"Better how?"

John had seen a show on serial killers that said if you keep them talking, you might live longer; besides, there didn't seem much else to do.

"Better because you so clearly fill the vacuum that he has left in my life."

"Maybe I could take his place as a living spouse."

"You could not bring to me what he brought to me."

"What did he bring?"

"Liberation. My father and mother were poor, not because of the million chances in India to be poor, they were poor by choice. They had chosen to give up their jobs at the university in a search for the truth. There isn't much money in truth."

"So Mason brought you money?"

"Money and love, and he wanted little in return."

"What did he want?"

"I am the one with the gun. I will ask the questions. Do you like my little gun? It's a twenty-two. Did you know that almost all professional hits are done with twenty-two? Not with three-fifty-sevens. A twenty-two at close range. The Uzi shoots a twenty-two-caliber bullet, of course it shoots so many of them that you only have to aim in the neighborhood so to speak."

"It's a lovely gun."

Oh Christ, thought John. *That may be my last sentence and I really said "It's a lovely gun."*

"Did Dr. Niles kill my husband?"

"I don't know how Dr. Niles fits into this."

"Why did you go to see Dr. Niles?"

"Because your slave from the restaurant told me to."

"You had no idea who he was, till I caused you to know?"

"No."

"Where were you when my husband was killed?"

"Sleeping in my bed if the time of death was right."

"And you heard nothing?"

"No. I thought you had a friend in the police department."

"Vincent told you everything, didn't he? Well I lied to Vincent about a great many things. That was what Mason always said do—'Create a fog about yourself.' I was the only one he was truthful to."

"How do you know that he was truthful to you?"

She slapped him across his face. He was tired and his toe ached so badly right now that the slap meant little. John was wondering if a bullet shot would really feel much worse.

"Of course he was truthful to me. He had no reason to lie to me. He and I were partners. Two horses yoked in tandem to do the Great Work."

"Well if you were partners, why don't you know what was going on?"

This entire discussion had taken very little time, but in John's mind hours had gone by. He expected at any minute Cassilda would be back to take him to the motel.

Chandra seemed a little ruffled for the first time.

"An assistant doesn't need to know what's going on. Do those women of yours know what's going on?"

"Probably, at least they know as much as I do, which isn't much. That's what makes them partners."

"Taylor shared almost everything with me, except at the

end. I need to know about the end. I need to know what he was trying."

"Well if you can spare me for a few days, perhaps we can figure it out."

"A nice try, but I have only a few minutes to decide whether to spare you; your woman is coming back. I don't want to kill her or be killed by her, it would spoil the symmetry of the thing."

"Well what can I do to facilitate your decision?"

"You can tell me about the last few weeks before my husband's death."

"Well I had been working on a series of short scenarios for an all-purpose FRP supplement, I had my seashell scenario, my false idols scenario, my magic newspaper scenario, and I was finishing up the text part of *Sethos 2*. I had had deadline fever—"

At this point she slapped him again. He grabbed for her, but she pulled back, pointing the gun at his face.

"I am not interested in your miserable line of work," she said. "I want to know about the tattoos."

"But I didn't get the tattoos in the last few weeks."

"No, Taylor got the tattoos in the last few weeks, when he went on that trip he wouldn't tell me about."

"The trip to Amarillo?"

"I don't know where he went, I just know that he went to find out about you."

"Why was he interested—"

Another slap.

"All right," said John. "He went to Amarillo to talk to my ex-wife."

"Keep talking."

"My ex-wife gave him some background on me. That's when he got the tattoos."

"What do they mean?"

"The one on my arm is for a mediocre rock group out of New Mexico called the Electric Luddites. They were sort of an eighties phenomenon. Mary Denning managed them."

"She managed a rock group?"

"Yeah, she and my wife were good friends. I wrote a song for them."

"What does the other one mean, the black rose on your heart?"

"Well that came from Mary as well. She told my wife that the symbol for love had always been the rose with its softness, its many layers, its sweet fragrance, its thorns. She said the perfect symbol of love would be a black rose, because that would show a love beyond the constraints of nature. Natural roses bloom and fade, their color is bright and holds no secrets. Immortal love fades not, and is filled with secrets. With immortal love there are a thousand virginities—"

"A thousand virginities to be lost, every night holding a new promise," finished Chandra. "I did not know that he had learned those words from Mary Denning. I thought they were his own. They are written inside of my wedding band. So you got the rose to symbolize your love for your wife?"

"Yes."

"And he got the rose to pass for you?"

"Yes, and to get more lessons from my ex-wife."

"Lessons?"

"She taught him how to make love like me."

"He slept with her?"

"Yes. She was so horny, and she only really trusts people that she has slept with."

"You are lying to me."

"I have no reason to lie."

"So he got this rose, this symbol of immortal love on his heart when he was sleeping with another woman?"

"Well, yes."

"You have killed me. I do not know who has killed my husband but you have killed me. Show me your rose."

John unbuttoned his shirt.

She tapped the rose with the fingers of her left hand while she pointed the gun at it with her right.

"He never touched me after his trip. Never once. He never told me what he had found out. He had always told me before. When he went to Tibet to see Dr. Zhang he told me, even though he was oath-bound not to reveal Zhang's formula for 'finding change points.' He told me. I could make millions of dollars on that. So you had this tattooed on your chest and you left your woman?"

"We couldn't work things out."

"This same woman that Mason slept with?"

"Yes."

"This woman told you all of this?"

"Yes."

"You love her now?"

"Yes."

"Because of Mason, you can love this woman that gave herself to him."

"She told me what she did. Sharing truth is more important as an act of love than fidelity."

"My parents said that. They were fools for the truth. You will make a perfect substitute for Mason. Close your eyes, relax, I won't miss."

"I would rather face death than have it come upon me."

"You are brave, but I may miss if I have to look at your face. I don't like your blond hair. Mason wasn't a blond."

"Maybe you can have my hair dyed posthumously."

"Close your eyes."

John did so. He felt the tiredness swallow him. Then he heard the sound that he had heard before.

Thunder spoke her name.

20 The Increase of Dust

He had not expected to look upon the world again. His views on the afterlife had always been a bit unfocused, but they did not include seeing Cassilda's face big and out of focus, the smell of cordite, and the shabby surroundings of Lone Star Games. Nothing hurt, except his goddamn toe. His hearing was gone again or Cassilda was indulging in a prank to make him think that was the case.

"What happened?" he asked.

He could see her mouthing words, but nothing came out. A gun lay on the counter. Chandra Mason's little gun. He looked to see if the bathroom door was open. *Who's afreud of the big bad dream?* Well for starters he was. Cassilda grabbed him. He could see her words on her lips, "Are you hurt?"

"I fainted. I don't hurt. My ears are out of commission."

He watched her lips again, "Do you want to go to the doctor?"

"I want to go home. I think she has left."

After some more lip-synching asking if he was sure, she

agreed to take him home, to the home of their marriage. If he didn't get his hearing back in an hour, she could take him to the doctor. She thought that this was a Bad Idea, he should go to the doctor now.

The door to his house, *their* house he kept thinking, was partially open, as it had been the morning he had found the double. He wondered if he walked in if he would find yet another copy of his self in an endless Xeroxage of Death. He still couldn't hear. Cassilda could be shouting warnings from behind him, or Chandra laughing some evil Kali cult laugh just beyond the door. He went in. He was tired of bullshit.

The front room was very dusty. He could feel the grit under his shoes as it ground against the wooden floor. The house smelled stale. There was something wrong about visiting his house like this. It was like seeing something by lantern light, a mystery of the Night that remained of the Night despite the minor light of day. It belonged to Hermes, who made you see the Night and tricked you into thinking it was the same as Day. He expected with each step for something to dart out and hurt him in this alien world.

There were dishes in the sink furry with white and black mold.

The refrigerator was a terrible place of corruption.

There were fast-food containers in front of the TV. The bed was messed up. There were ropes on the bed. His office was untouched, but covered in dust.

It was far too dusty, he thought, for the brief time he was away. Another trick, he decided, a trick to make him lose track of time. The only thing that would be left, he decided, was his own knowledge that he existed and that he had been changed.

He was the constant, everything else the variable.

He turned on his computer.

Cassilda was running through the house checking every closet, behind every sofa.

The screen that he had been typing on the last day of his work came up. A stupid scenario (perhaps even stupider than *Sethos 2*) that he had a smaller copy of on his laptop. He plunked a few more characters on the last line of it.

SEASHELL: The Story

> You find a nautilus shell on a small sandy beach at the base of great dark cliffs. When you place the shell near your ear and listen, you hear it speak:
> When we first entered the Cave of Winds, we found this miraculous enchanted shell. It repeats what is spoken into it. At first we treated it as a curiosity, but now I have decided to record how the Umma-beasts attacked us. When I have finished speaking into this shell, I will throw it into the fast-moving stream that flows through the Cave. I hope that some future seekers learn from our failure and obtain the great treasures we sought.
> My name is Asatron Vindor. My group of ten men had heard that mysterious beasts guarded splendid treasure in the caves overlooking the sea. We armed ourselves as any group greedy for gold might and climbed the cliffs. Inside the cave, Dwandor Yoorsson, our leader, found this shell. He placed it to his ear and heard the

roaring of the Umma-Beasts. He turned a small key and the shell stopped speaking, and after a few minutes of play he induced it to speak with his voice. We all tried it and were amazed at how strange our voices sounded. Near the shell was a small pile of gold dust, which I gathered up—surely it was a sign of the gods' favor.

We descended into the cave. Soon we saw that although the cave appeared natural, perhaps carved by the fast-flowing stream at its center, it was in reality a cleverly disguised artificial lair. We passed through room after room, each smaller than before— not unlike the chambers of this nautilus. Suddenly we heard the awful roaring of the beasts behind us. We recognized the sounds we had first heard from the shell. Ummas! We ran farther into the labyrinth.

We came at last to this innermost chamber. Here lies the wealth of ages. Strange vessels of mother-of-pearl, carvings of coral, indeed every art you can imagine from the mysteries of the sea. But we scarcely looked upon this bounty before the small green horrors fell upon us. Vindor loosed his magics; A-ron, the elven warrior, shot his arrows with the speed and accuracy that had won him renown; and I swung my sword. Our blows rained down upon them, the magics found their target—yet to no avail.

I alone remain. My wounds shall claim me, and the Umma-beasts will no doubt gloat over my body, but perhaps if I spread the news that these sea beasts have a weakness for gold dust, perhaps new warriors will come to the Cave of the Winds. Perhaps you may bury me and my comrades, and carry away the rich and strange sea-treasure. I hear the Umma-beasts in the corridor beyond. I must throw the shell into the water. May the Passions grant that it finds worthy seekers. . . .

SEASHELL: Gaming Notes

HOOK

* The PCs, seeking the naiad from [THE PREVIOUS SCENARIO], find a nautilus shell on the beach. It speaks the "Seashell" legend in a gruff, stagy voice, as though reading a text.

* A dwarven craftsman rushes out of his shop, briefly panicked. "Was just readyin' to saw through a shell for a mosaic, when all over sudden it started talkin'! Dropped it and ran, I did.—What? You're interested? Twenty gold and you can take it away." Characters can bargain him down to 2 gold pieces. The dwarf bought the shell months ago at the local marketplace, but cannot remember from whom.

SPEAKER
The tiger-stripe nautilus shell
measures a hand-span in diameter
and four inches thick. About as
fragile as a china plate.

STORY
The shell's story leads players
to a cave, outfitted with numerous
secret passages along its sides.
The treasure of the sea-people is
there, as well as a group of
enterprising dwarves. Q

The whole idea was to lure people to waste their time tracking down the cave. There weren't any Umma-beasts, just some dwarves that made talking seashells. The dwarves caught people who were trying to get rich quick. It was an elaborate fake treasure map, but if the players outsmarted the dwarves they got a huge treasure—all the lot the dwarves had got over the years. So the fake map was a real map. There was a lesson here, he decided; he was writing this for himself. It was just as real seeming as his house was.

He could begin to hear Cassilda speaking.

"Do you hear me now? What happened?" she asked.

"Thunder," he said. "When we were tossed out of the garden. Thunder saying, 'You better figure it out for yourself.' "

"You're delirious."

"On the contrary, I am quite focused and battle ready. What is a Man? Man is the Increase of Dust, Mighty is the hawk's talon-span."

"I am taking you to the hospital."

"No, just let me sleep. I have a false treasure map to follow, and I need a clearer mind to be fooled in the right way. I've just ridden back to town after being away for years, and I've got to rid the homes of the false idols."

"Oh God, you've lost it. You've only been gone for five or six days."

"No. It may look that to the outer world, but in here"— John tapped his head—"in here it has been years. I've got to use this reality for my clues for a while. That's where my enemies are working, my friends too. Let me sleep."

He made his way to the bed and pushed off the ropes. He was asleep before his head hit the pillow.

When he awoke the house smelled fresh. Cassilda had aired out the house. The ringing was gone from his ears, his big toe wasn't throbbing, and he could hear Cassilda and Michelle in another room. He felt peaceful and the feverish thoughts he had held before his keyboard were gone, or at least almost gone. The treasure map. That was interesting. He wondered for a moment if he could recast his whole thinking on the incident. What if this whole thing had been (and still was) an *opportunity* to gain something? Dad had had a chance to make money with silver in Brazil, and then had had another opportunity. Maybe this was his big break in some strange way. If he could only piece it all together. He needed to stop being afreud of the big bad dream. It all hinged on *why* Mason had gone to such lengths to look like him. There had to be some good thing coming his way. If he stopped reacting and started acting, then he could grab it with both hands when it came his way. That seemed to be Dr. Niles's message, but he couldn't tell if Niles was a bad guy or a good guy. He had to assume Mason was a bad guy, because if he was a good guy and had been trying to save John from an awful fate, that meant John was really in for it.

And then there's the three men.

The women's voices weren't quite loud enough for him to

hear. There was love and concern in their voices. Love for him, John realized. He hadn't paid much attention to love. Was there really anyone as loved as he was? He had the love of the two women in the front room, and the love of his mom, who would be arriving with a four-wheel-drive vehicle full of guns tomorrow trying to turn everything into a western novel.

Oh Jesus. Better have something for Mom and Henry to do. Something real, but something or they would shoot up everything and everybody. Somehow that had never been a worry of his over the years. He hadn't ever worried about Mom's shoot-'em-up tendencies, but he guessed people changed in their late seventies.

God he felt good.

There was no reason why he should feel good, except that love thing. He had no reason to assume that Chandra Mason was out of his life, that the three men weren't following him around, or that he would find out about Dr. Niles and his father. But he felt like Mom was baking chocolate cake or Dad was taking him to Palo Duro Canyon that day. He looked at the clock. Five in the afternoon. Probably time to get one more piece of the puzzle before dark. He wasn't going to do flashlight reality tonight. He wasn't going to do motels. He was going to stay in this house and begin the work of making it his own again.

He smelled bad, but he would take care of that later.

He walked into the front room. The women watched him with a mixture of fear and concern.

"That's where I found the body," John said, pointing to a section of the floor. "A false idol."

"See?" said Cassilda in a loud whisper to Michelle.

"Oh I'm sane now. I know a hake from a handsaw," said John. "You have to go through a period of unsane between sane without knowing and sane with knowing," said John.

"And what do you know?" said Michelle.

"I know that I'm in a play. I'm in a game to make me think certain thoughts at certain times. I'm just not sure who the author is, or authors are. I don't know the winning conditions. All I lack is a one-nine-hundred number for game hints. But I guess I know where that might be. I want to go to Dr. Niles's house."

"You think someone's there?" asked Cassilda.

"I am hoping some**thing's** there. That's the way I would design it if this were a game scenario. A clue, a hidden cache with some treasure in it. A magic stone perhaps, or the Graal."

"Wouldn't that mean you had won if you found the Graal?" asked Cassilda.

"Not yet," said John. "I don't know what question to ask, at least not exactly."

They drove in Michelle's car.

John told Cassilda to stay in the car with the motor running. It had after all worked as a plan thirteen hours ago. John walked in and Michelle followed. The small stucco house seemed empty. The wall was whiter where paintings had been, the carpet less faded where a sofa had rested. They went into the kitchen where the dining table remained. There was a small key on the table that John picked up and put in his pocket.

Nothing in the two bedrooms except for a couple of dead palmetto bugs and the little car from a Monopoly game. John pocketed that as well. There was a small utility room at the back. There were still a washer and a dryer, which John felt around all the cracks of. He came up with a stiff mildewed-smelling sock from the washer.

"Ah I know something that Niles doesn't. Wherever he is, I bet he's wondering where this sock went."

Michelle laughed.

John said, "I guess I've wasted our time. I felt like I knew something."

"There's still the garage," said Michelle.

They went outside. The garage door had a rusty padlock. John reached into his pocket for the key and pulled out the little car while Michelle pulled at the lock, which popped open.

The garage was full of junk, empty paint cans, old tires, rusty tools, baling wire, sacks of concrete, half-empty sacks of chemical fertilizer. Along the wall someone had nailed each license plate he had ever had.

Then Michelle saw the box.

It was the same box from her vision.

But it wasn't between two candles, it wasn't on a niche in an ancient hall. It was just a little wooden dirty box sitting on a paint can.

"Here," she said. "This is it."

She picked it up.

"You folks thinking of buying?" A woman had walked up the driveway behind them. Michelle hid the box behind her purse.

"Yes, ma'am," said John. "What sort of neighborhood is this?"

"Quiet and no shenanigans," she said.

"Well that's exactly what I'm looking for," said John. "I am John Lalor and this is my wife, Sarah May Lalor, and out in the car is my emergency blowout wife, Susareen Lalor. Now you do still hold the tradition of the lottery here, don't you? Not like those valley folk?"

The middle-aged woman at the end of the driveway began making movements with her mouth, like a fish out of water. John started walking toward her. Michelle followed and she retreated to her home.

"Enough shenanigans for one day," said John. They got in the car and drove home.

On the way Michelle opened the box. It was full of tissue paper and a 3.5-inch diskette.

21 The History of the Brotherhood of Travelers

The disk was yellow and had a word written on it in green Magic Marker. WASTE, a little homage to Pynchon, John thought. It had twenty-four files, and each required a password to open it. W.A.S.T.E. opened the twenty-first file.

```
THE HISTORY OF THE BROTHERHOOD OF
TRAVELERS
Prepared as an entrance exam by
David Robert Niles for Inspector
Yage Raoul Tomas

    The Brotherhood extends back
into the dimmest section of human
history beginning with the
migrations of the last Ice Age. It
was there that humans developed
the cognitive fluidity that made
them masters of the various
specialized intelligences that
evolution had provided the
species. This change came with
```

changing environments, that is to say, Travel.

However, the modern documentable beginning of the Brotherhood began with Ibn Batua. A young devout Muslim, he began the hajj on June 14, 1325. He traveled from Tangier (which is why it is one of the sacred cities of our Order) to Mecca with a side trip to Baghdad. After studying the holy Koran for three years in Mecca, he made his trip to East Africa, followed by a journey up the eastern littoral of the Mediterranean. At Ephesus he purchased a beautiful Greek slave girl named Sophia. She took him to see the ruins of the second largest library of the Antique World; they looked upon the statues of Arete, Eunoia, and Sophia that Apulia had erected in this library memorial to his father, Tiberius Julius Caesar. She told him the story of Jason and the Argonauts, and he then decided to repeat their journey across the Black Sea, to the Ukraine, down to Istanbul, and then east to the Volga. He traveled along the icebound river several hundred miles north, but unable to find golden fleece among the fur traders, went south to far Samarkand and on to the Indus.

There he obtained employment with Sultan Tughlaq. Tughlaq made him the ambassador to China. He left for China by sea, but a terrible storm destroyed everyone aboard the many ships (he was traveling with a huge company of foot soldiers) except for Sophia and him. Like Odysseus they washed up on a friendly beach, and he became a kazi in the Maldive Islands. After an attempt to introduce Islam to the natives failed, he set off for India seeking his old employer, but the ship was blown off course and he landed in Ceylon. For nine days as his ship neared the island, he could see Mount Sarandib, and after establishing himself with the local sultan, one of his first explorations was to go to the mountain.

There he found what he believed to be a huge footprint in the dark basalt. The print was eleven spans in length and he took it to be the footprint of Adam, beginning his journey out of Eden. There was a small Buddhist shrine nearby and it was there he found an ancient scroll written in Greek which he bought from the monks. Sophia was able to translate the scroll and it became the founding document of our Order (see below).

While she was at work translating the *Krypticon* (for the scroll was so entitled), he left again for India, and again bad luck struck. Captured by pirates, he lost his wives and jewels. Only he and Sophia were spared. Working with only his knowledge of foreign lands and Sophia's linguistic ability, he once again acquired a fortune and made his way to Java, where an old friend from the court of Tughlaq got him a job as an ambassador to China (once again), but this time he got to go to Peking. This is an Illustration of the Principle of Similarity— whatever comes into being in your life will produce similar results again and again—even when these events come from "chance."

He began the study of the *Krypticon*, which Sophia had rendered into Arabic and was disturbed thereby, and went again into the Muslim world hoping to regain the surety of his faith. He went first to his homeland of Morocco, arriving in November of 1349. He had been away for twenty-four years, which is why twenty-four is a sacred number for our Order. But like Ulysses he became restless, first heading off to Spain to join in a war there (that set up for the events of 1492), but mainly for the thrill of passing beyond the Pillars of Hercules.

He returned to Morocco, and getting a job with the sultan, he and Sophia journeyed south to Mali. He had seen in his life the Nile, the Tigris, the Volga, the Indus, the Yellow River, and now the Niger. After establishing diplomatic relations with Mali he returned to Morocco and settled in Fez (which is the second holy city of our Order) and thereupon wrote his book *Travels in Asia and*

Africa. By this time he had traveled seventy-five thousand miles, a feat which Batua scholar Evan S. Connell says "makes the journeys of Marco Polo look like a stroll around the block."

It was reported by Batua's biographer Hafiz ib Najjar that after Batua had lived in Fez for twenty-four years, he one day appeared at court seeming restored to his youth. He announced that he was going to travel to a land in the west and visit two great rivers. The sultan ordered him to reveal his secret of rejuvenation, but Batua said he could not speak them, for only by traveling could one discover the secret. But in order to please the sultan he left a practical translation of the *Krypticon,* which he had retitled *al-Futuhat al-Sarandibah (The Sarandib Revelations).* It is believed that he visited the Mississippi and his visit seems to be recorded in the mythology of the Choctaw, Chickasaw, Yazoo, and Pascagoula tribes. His last quest was to the Amazon, and despite the story of his immortality, there is a small tomb erected there. I visited the tomb in the forties and saw the legend carved in Greek, "My Name is written in my journey." I attest that this is as true as the truism that the Pope doeth poopeth in Ye Woods.

David R. Niles

The Sarandib Revelations

If a copy of this Book is kept by the Traveler he cannot be slain by brigands, nor destroyed by storm or fire, nor withered by old age as long as he continues his journey. This is the book that Bion wrote when he traveled from Ethiopia to Hyperborea and then to the Pillars of Hercules and then left as an offering to the ever-striding god at the shrine of the footprint for the one destined to pick it up.

Above Thebes and Hermonthis, above Silsia and Ombos, Bion had ascended the Nile. He had even passed the Elephantine Isle where the territory of Egypt ends, and had advanced toward black Ethiopia, which is close to the end of the world.

He had no boat with which to overcome the slow course of the river, for he would have needed slaves to handle the oars and he was apprehensive of depending on disinterested companions. Therefore he journeyed on foot along the damp, grassy banks so narrow that his path sometimes ran along the foot of the multicolored cliffs from which stretched back the monotonous infinity of the Desert.

The narrow band of living earth is all the Traveler needs, and woe to him who finds it not but sleeps among the sands.

He came to a region unlike his native Ithaca, where his great-great-grandsire Odysseus had departed from in his last journey. Ostriches and giraffes ran over the distant wastes; herds of antelopes fled like yellow clouds; monkeys hung suspended in fantastic groups from the supple branches of sycamores; and occasionally in the mud of the Nile, where the slender steps of hermes birds followed each other like long flowers, Bion contemplated the formidable human imprint left by the mysterious Amanit, the beast upon which no man dared look but of which the Ethiopians told strange stories. And

Bion, uneasy, was persuaded that the Colossi of rose granite, sculptured in the mass of the mountains, came in solitary nights to bathe themselves in the holy river which is the father of all.

Bion came at last to the land of the oldest of men, who lived in mud huts behind their date palms, fearing the creatures of the night, and he dwelt among these people for a season. He asked if they knew where his great-great-grandsire had traveled. And they knew not of this, but one the chief of them persuaded Bion to spend the night with the youngest of his two daughters, who had not yet known a man. Bion was not unfamiliar with this custom and he venerated it as a tradition of singular virtue. The gods often visited earth dressed as Travelers, soldiers, or shepherds, and who could distinguish a mortal from an Olympian who did not wish to reveal himself? Bion was, perhaps, Hermes?

The young one came to him with much trembling and paleness, and was received by him in the darkness of the Night.

He began his walk to the north. If his great-great-grandsire had not sought the South, perhaps the land of Eternal Day held his great-great-grandsire—or at least his tomb upon which might be written the secrets of the world gained after so much questing.

But he was overtaken by the young one, who ran as fleet as a gazelle. She wore nothing but tears.

"Why are you here, child?" he asked.

"I came to follow thee, to remain with thee always, always . . ."

"Child, I pleasured you last night, I have made you ready for men as is the custom of your people. Return home to the house of your father."

But she clung to him.

He threw her aside saying, "I cannot take a companion

now, I am on a quest to last a lifetime. You will suffer much from me. Go now."

But she ran alongside of him and said, "I shall go where thou goest, I loved thee yesterday as I do today; I had never loved anyone; I love only thee. Oh, I shall love only thee."

And Bion struck her down, yet she stood and proceeded along with him. He resolved not to speak to her at any time, hoping that she would lose her faith and return. As they came to a city he took his cloak and clothed her, lest the inhabitants do some harm to her.

He sought to leave in the hours before dawn, but she had risen likewise and was his traveling companion. And he spoke to her only of the terrors of the journey.

When he came at last to Cairo, he forbade her to follow him, but she said to him, "I cannot leave thee. Do not drive me away. I do not ask to be a wife since thou refusest to love me. I beg thee, let me stay near thee. I shall belong to thee. Make anything of me. I will be thy slave, if thou wishest."

And he told her that she was his slave.

And the next day he sold her to a wandering chief of the plains.

He journeyed north to the land of Eternal Day, and there he saw great white bears swimming in an ocean of black, and the sky shimmer with a rainbow bridge at Night, and men climbed up ladders to be with the gods. But they knew not of his great-great-grandsire. So he returned again to his home and resolved to try the ultimate West. He gathered up a great ship and with many men set to follow the sun's setting although it was forbidden to do so, and he came to the Pillars of Hercules beyond which no man may travel, and he found there his ancestor's name carved upon the rock and a single arrow pointing farther west.

He set forth, and each day his crew grew more fearful waiting for Poseidon to send his kraken to slay them for their impiety. At last a great storm did come and all save he were taken to the deep to sit and serve the misty god.

But Bion was washed ashore on an island of the West, and there the people took him into slavery, for they knew not the laws of Zeus. And he served as a slave to a forester for ten years, till one day when the forester took him to the great city called Atalantide. There he saw the great capital and heard stories of the witch queen who ruled the land by sorcery.

He said to the forester, "O master have I not served you better than any of your slaves?"

The forester agreed it was so.

"Then O master, I beg thee a boon, sell me to the Witch Queen. She will pay you well for me, and I will have a chance to learn if she knows of my great-great-grandsire."

This was done and he worked about the palace a year before coming into the presence of the Queen.

When he saw her, he knew it was the woman he had sold into slavery, and she looking at him knew him.

"O foolish man!" she cried out. "If you had but loved me, my destiny would long ago have taken you here, for it is on this island that the tomb of your great-great-grandsire is built, and I who alone know its secret do rule this island by the power of my knowing."

He fell to the ground.

"Thou speakest the truth for the most evil thing I did was spurn thy love. For the Traveler must learn to see that the gifts Fate gives him are the keys to the hidden doors. You may do with me as you like, and extract your vengeance as you desire."

She had him chained to a wall and took a great whip and he knew that she would whip him to death, and that this was fair.

But she only struck him once and then declared that the punishment was complete.

"You are now free, because my destiny caused me to be sold from chieftain to more chieftain. So skilled I became in the arts of love that at last I was sold to the King of Atalantide, who ruled by alone knowing the secret of the tomb of Odysseus. My lover the King Clinias died before we had offspring, and he gave me the secret."

He laid himself before her saying, "Then of my free will I am become yours if thou will but have me. Each day I have regretted my action which I thought would spare you the agonies of my quest. Yet I realize that the love of someone as pure as thee was what I was in fact questing for."

"Rise then and be my love."

She took him that night to the tomb of Odysseus. There were writings painted upon the tomb in the picture writing of Atalantide, which he knew not. A great god was shown striding through the Desert. In his left hand he held a scroll that was but partially written upon, and he read the scroll with half a glance and kept the other upon the horizon. In his right hand he held a key fashioned like the cross of the Egyptians.

She then told him the secret of the painting, which may only pass from mouth to ear, and he took an Oath to pass it along to others who had suffered as much as she had suffered but to no others.

She told him then, that her rulership was not a form of great freedom as she had dreamt of its being. She was a slave although a slave who wore the finest silks and the richest jewels. She could not leave the island, nor love whom she wished, nor even eat as she wished. Her one desire was to flee from the West.

With great stealth did Bion and she plot. He began working as a free man in the city taking up the skill of boatbuilding, for the people of Atalantide did trade with an uncouth folk farther to the West, and boatbuilders were well thought of. The Atalantidens were not as skilled in this craft as the Greeks, and he taught them much but not all that he had learned.

When he had built a small fast boat, he asked the Queen to come and inspect it. Persuading the harbormaster that he was not leaving the great bay, he was allowed to take the Queen on a small journey. At the edge of the ocean he put his boat to full sail.

Their crafts could not overtake the brine-steed, for in their peaceful kingdom they had not mastered the ebb and flow of water, which is life itself, and soon their queen was far away.

But ever did Bion and his Queen, whose name was Foresight, look to spies from the West who might seek to reclaim her. So they journeyed to the ultimate East and left there this book before striding into another world. This book is but a comment to what they told the men of the Shrine of the Footprint, which is repeated among travelers' tales to this day.

22 Henry's Tale

"**Well, that helps a** whole fucking lot," said Michelle.

"Verily as the Pope doeth poopeth in ye woods," agreed Cassilda.

It was late, time for bed. After locking the doors of his house John decided to crash. Michelle didn't want to spend the night at her apartment just yet, so John gave the two women his bed, and he slept on the sleeper couch in the front room; as he folded out the bed he realized that his feet would be over the spot where Mason had lain. Or if he slept with his feet toward the couch, his head would be.

He decided to do this as a sign of trying to get into the head of Taylor Keziah Mason. He expected wondrous dreams and great revelations, but so swiftly and soundly did he sleep that he thought it a dream when Cassilda was shaking him awake. She had a package of Dunkin' Donuts glazed black and orange. Halloween was after all tomorrow night.

Michelle had started coffee, and they discussed the arrival of Elaine and Henry.

"My biggest fear is that they'll get their fool selves hurt," said John.

"I don't know what they can get hurt on. It's all over. Chandra seems to be out of the picture, and Dr. Niles has moved away except for leaving us the diskette, which has nothing to do with dead men in the living room. We just need to decide how to get along with our lives, which will begin first with John deciding what he wants, and then the rest of us deciding what we want, and ending our various sick leaves and vacations going on now."

"I wonder if Niles left the diskette?" asked John.

"Of course he left it," said Cassilda.

"But how did he know we'd find it?" asked Michelle. "I mean we found it because of a vision."

"Well maybe he can send dreams—That was a standard part of magical technology in late antiquity. But, if you ask me, it's a well-conceived prank. I got screwed by a landlord once, the guy wouldn't fix anything and so forth. So I wrote a fake diary in a little spiral notebook about how the house was haunted, and I left it in the attic of the house when I moved out. Now I don't know if the new tenants ever found the book and got spooked. I noticed the next people didn't stay very long. Besides, your vision was of a stone-lined hall with candles, not a crap-filled garage in Hyde Park."

"The box looked the same," said Michelle.

"You're not listening to me. I didn't ask about the hows of leaving the diskette, I asked about the whys. Why did he do it?" asked John.

"It is either a genuine initiatory text, a hoax, or proof that our mysterious friend had too much time on his hands," said Cassilda.

"It will either help you figure out what's going on, or waste your time like nobody's business," added Michelle.

"Maybe both," said John. "Playing chess doesn't help you with your life problems, but if you can generalize the game—say for example its strategies for beginning, middle, and endgame into ways of problem solving—then you've got certain tools for life."

"Yeah, but you don't give someone a chess set in the middle of a problem," said Cassilda.

"Well like you said," said John, "maybe the problem is over right now, maybe this is the brooding stage."

"At least until Elaine and Henry arrive at four o'clock," said Cassilda.

Michelle left soon after to spend the day at work, promising to drop by in the evening. Cassilda helped John clean up; after all was said and done it was still Mom coming to visit her bachelor son. They worked well together, like old times when they had been in sync, when their bodies knew the signals of each other, little needed to be said, and laughter became frequent, such as when Cassilda merely arched an eyebrow at the mountain of unmatched socks.

When four o'clock came near, John asked Cassilda, "Why do you think Chandra is out of the picture?"

"I think she is like the slave girl in the story, firing the gun at you rather than into you as her one lash of the whip."

"But that model does not apply," said John. "Foresight whipped the man who had bought her and abandoned her."

"Yeah, but he wasn't around. You're just his placeholder."

The Ford Explorer rolled in behind John's Taurus.

Elaine and Henry bounded out and there was a four-person dance of carrying in suitcases, rifles, food, going to the rest room, throwing away snack wrappings, giving and getting hugs, getting sodas, inquiries about the trip and the road and the weather, questions about routes and plans for dinner.

Before long they were at Tong Jing enjoying the buffet.

John took his mom through it, explaining each dish. Michelle arrived and joined the extended family group. John told them about Chandra and the diskette.

Henry said, "I have some thoughts on that key thing. I began work as a key cutter, one of those little men in kiosks. I worked outside of the Sears Roebuck store on the corner of Dixie and Plains. Since I was sort of trapped there, I had to put up with occasional weirdos. I remember back in 1976, while I was watching the tall ships come into New York Harbor on my little black-and-white TV, a little guy with a Hitler mustache came to the kiosk. He wanted me to join an all-powerful brotherhood of key makers. He had this pamphlet that showed the crossed keys of the Manx Parliament and had an acrostic legend:

"**K**eep on your toes for lucky breaks!

"**E**ven the seeming bum may be made a King!

"**Y**ou must Teach to all who ask!

"**M**any may knock, but most are locked out!

"**E**very little bit helps!

"**N**ow is the time!

"The little guy couldn't explain the group very well, but it consisted of six practices. One, an agreement not to infringe on each other's territory. Two, sending two percent of gross profits to someone in Dunwich, Massachusetts, called the Gate, the Key, and the Guardian of the Gate. Three, participating in a Great Books reading program and taking the fruits of that program to our customers. Four, keeping a copy of every key we made (I guess for illicit purposes). Five, doing random good deeds on certain 'Key' days. And six, helping each other out kind of like the Masons. 'Our lives are Keys to Doors we only see way too late,' he said. He had a few other goofier aphorisms than that about the Keymen. I never knew if he was the only one of these guys, and thereby hoping to double his membership, or if there was some vast cabal infiltrating key cutters around the world. He said it was the latter—always telling me about keymen in Moscow and Honolulu and Sydney or Mr. Jaggers in British Intelligence. I let him hang around as long as he didn't bother customers. You can get pretty bored sitting in a kiosk waiting for some housewife to copy her house keys for her kids. Most of the key cutters I knew got into UFOs, or conspiracy theory, or drinking. Anyway one day he just didn't show up. I never knew what happened, but the weird thing is what he tried to sell me sort of worked. I did sign up for one of those Great Book study programs, 'From Plato to Sartre' I think it was called, which I stuck with for four years and I did try doing a random good deed every six days—you know, little stuff like jumping someone's car or giving blood or something. I figure that makes me a 'key man' in lots of people's lives. I like to fantasize that there are folks who got to meet their loved ones because I jumped their car, or got over being homeless because I gave them a handout. Now probably it don't matter a damn, but it makes me feel good."

It was then that the Three Men entered the restaurant. The three men were white, and their suits were actually a dark charcoal gray. Black ties, white shirts, black shades, clean-cut, and still a little too pasty, John decided.

They took a table next to John's. All conversation ceased. Elaine left the table to powder her nose.

One of the three looked over at John's table.

"Oh Mr. Reynman what a coincidence, we're going to call on you tomorrow. Since we have luckily run into you, perhaps you can join us for a moment."

John crossed to their table.

As before in bad melodrama fashion the three men alternated in speaking. They were so clearly the embodiment of anti-individuality that John never once thought of them as people. His mind fantasized about hive-mind aliens from fifties sci-fi.

"What were you going to see me about?" asked John.

"We noticed that you made a trip right after we saw you."

"A brief trip, I'm back, less than two weeks away. I hope you have been busy."

There was a loud backfire on the parking lot.

"We are always, but Mr. Reynman, the world is always about to crack into a million pieces, our job is to cement those cracks together, fill in the little holes that chaos might slip through. You understand that, Mr. Reynman, you have to fill in cracks in those games you write, all sorts of beta testing."

"What holes are there in your games, gentlemen?"

Two of the three were rising to get some food.

Cassilda walked over and said, "John, we need to go."

The remaining man said, "Please Ms. Jones we will only need Mr. Reynman for a few minutes."

Nice subtle threat, the dropping of a name.

Cassilda walked back to their table.

The three men talked about the weather, what a mild October it was, what a big holiday Halloween was for Austin and so forth. A couple more backfires had occurred outside. Elaine returned from the bathroom. John was growing tired of the game, and was about to leave, when real questions appeared again.

"We know that Mrs. Chandra Mason stayed in your home during your trip to Amarillo. We need to know the nature of your relationship with her."

"She and I are both seekers for the truth. That puts us at odds," said John.

"We don't follow."

"There is only so much truth out there. You can't share it with everybody. It has to be quested for," said John.

"Truth is limitless, and it is free."

"If it were free, then you wouldn't have to be asking me questions about Mrs. Mason. I've got a question for you: Who the hell was Taylor Keziah Mason, that you remotely give a damn?"

"We're here to ask questions."

"I thought you were here to enjoy the good Chinese food. The shrimp egg foo yung is particularly good tonight."

"We can make things very unpleasant for you."

"How? I've been shot at, my loved ones have been threatened, and worst of all for a freelancer, I've had an enforced vacation. You will do what exactly—inflict your poor dress sense on me?"

"We have our ways."

"My country is being defended by bad movie Nazis. If you want something from me, give something to me."

The three looked at one another.

"OK we'll say this—his mathematics were important to us. He was working on certain aspects of mapping that could be used in espionage."

John pondered this for a while.

"Like mapping one's self into another person? That would make quite the perfect spy. Why would he pick me as a guinea pig?"

"We don't know. But we will find out."

"Well if you do, please fucking tell me."

"Where is Chandra Mason?"

"She's looking for her husband's killer. Frankly, I think you guys are pretty high on her list."

"If her husband was killed at all."

"What the hell does that mean?"

"We think you are Taylor Keziah Mason. We think you knew that the agency wouldn't allow you to act on your own. You had used most of the huge fortune you had got from your data compression algorithms, so you picked a likely target to try your theories on."

"You have me there," said John. "Who better to transmigrate into than a game designer who makes twenty-four thou a year?"

"You could do the fairly infantile work, and then afterward you could make big bucks on some other piece of computer design. You did help things along by soaking your fingers in acid to remove the prints, but we knew you were in Austin. It was because of us that the police found your name at all—you had done great work in making yourself disappear from the world. Even your high school in Salem lacked any record of your existence."

"Well I have to hand it to you guys, I did such a good job that even I don't remember it."

"That was what we expected, but we can make you remember."

At this point Detective Anthony R. Blick and two plainclothes policemen entered the restaurant.

Detective Blick went directly to the table. Michelle got up to join them.

Detective Blick asked, "Mr. Rodgers, are you the owner of a disabled black '96 Cadillac Seville license number BHG28K?"

One of the three said, "I have a Cadillac, but it is not disabled."

"It is against the regulations of the city of Austin to leave a disabled vehicle on a public parking lot. I'm afraid I will have to arrange the towing of the vehicle now, and I need you to either pay for this service or accompany these officers downtown."

"You can't do this. I'll have your badge for this."

"Trying to obstruct a police official in the course of his lawful actions is a crime, Mr. Rodgers."

One of the other men put his hand on Rodgers's arm.

Detective Blick continued, "I noticed several violations of the vehicle code with the disabled Cadillac. Perhaps you would like to accompany the officers outside to inspect the vehicle."

"I certainly would. I think we all would."

The three men rose and left.

Blick looked at Reynman. "I got a call that there were three strange men here driving a Cadillac that had all four tires shot out. People like them should be much more careful."

"Thanks, but why are you helping out?"

"When those bozos showed up in my office thirteen days ago, I gave in. I totally bowed my head in the presence of a higher power. That kind of blind obedience is the road to dictatorship. It has bugged me ever since. All I am doing is returning the favor of harassment to them. If I work hard at it, I can probably lock them up for a day or so, but mainly I cut down on the sleaze factor and the cheap psychological warfare gimmicks. They don't know squat, and some psych has convinced them to play-act with people. Not on my watch."

"Thanks. This may mean more trouble for both of us, but it was everything to hear you scare them."

" 'To protect and to serve,' that's our motto. Call me tomorrow and I'll tell you what I know," said Detective Anthony R. Blick. "You're not of the woods yet."

23 You Are My Sunshine

John, Henry, and Elaine had gone to the Motel 6 where Henry and Elaine were staying.

John asked his mother for the seventh time, "What were you thinking that you shot out their tires?"

His mother sighed and said again, "I wanted to harass them. They were harassing you and that bothered me."

"Actually Mom, they weren't harassing me at all. I was getting information from them."

"Well I didn't know that. I left too early. Next time I'll wait awhile before I shoot people's tires."

"I think she did very well," said Henry, his arm around Elaine. "Calling that detective was brilliant."

"It was lucky that he hated those guys too," said John.

"No, that was easy to figure out. John had hated them, and any policeman in his right mind doesn't want feds playing mind games around him."

"How do you know that?" asked John.

"I watch TV," said Elaine. "I knew when he got a tip on

them and a chance to harass them he would, if he had any gumption."

"And if he didn't?"

"Well we could have left the restaurant at any time, and they wouldn't have followed."

"What are you guys going to do here?"

"We'll stay through the second. If anything is going to happen it will be on Halloween night," said Henry.

"How do you figure?"

"It's a big holiday here. My son went to school at UT. All of those masks, all of those people pretending to be someone that they're not—it's all too resonant with your situation, and besides, I overheard what the policeman told you."

"As much as I love you guys, and want you around, I don't want you shooting up Cadillacs."

"No, but you may want us calling the police. I do have a cell phone, and you've got to admit we look pretty out of the flow," said Henry.

"I'm seventy-six, you're seventy-five—we are out of the flow. This is, sadly, as close to the action as we are going to get," said Elaine.

"Well, I am dubious." said John.

"Be dubious, then. Halloween works out to be one of my 'key' days. I've got to find something good to do. If it's just watching your house, I'll do that." said Henry.

"I want to know about Niles, and I want to know what that has to do with the dead man. I am not spry enough to follow you on your quest, but I can watch your back and hand you cookies when you are done," said Elaine.

There were more pleasantries, and then John drove home.

Both women were there. Michelle still didn't feel like returning to her apartment, or maybe (John surmised) she didn't want to leave John alone with Cassilda.

John told them the three men's theory of his being Mason. It bothered him. What if such a thing could be true? What if Mason were hiding *inside* of him somewhere in the endless corridors of dreams that Cassutto talked about in *The Way Out*? Cassutto had argued that imagination was largely empty. The goal of life was to create vast empty spaces in which big thought could be thought. All of life was needed for this purpose, and occupations that increased the space of imagination were to be sought out. Maybe Mason really did want him because he was a game designer, maybe the use of imagination was what the guy had been after. Maybe that was why he did so many dumb things at the beginning of the process, he was misled by an alien spirit within him.

"Golyadkin," said Cassilda. "The hero of Dostoyevsky's *The Double*. A minor civil servant who develops a split personality. He believes there is another man who looks just like him. Let's see, that was written in 1846, one hundred and fifty-two years ago."

Michelle knocked on John's head. "Is there anybody in there? Come out, come out whoever you are!"

"Don't do that!" said John grabbing her hand, suddenly mad and scared. "I'm serious here, I'm scared."

"It suits the season," said Cassilda. "It is the grinning skulls in the convenience stores, it is the ghosts our neighbor across the street has hung up, there is a double world right now, a scary half world with its witches and goblins, walking skeletons and vampires. We haven't even bought any candy for tomorrow night. Does Allan still throw that party with his juggling friends?"

"Oh yeah, he had called me and left a message, I need to call him back. Do we want to go?"

"We being who?" asked Michelle.

"Well the three of us. I mean that's sort of awkward," said John. "I guess I need to pick one of you."

"Oh that's awfully egotistical, it's all up to you," said Cassilda.

"Well no I didn't mean it like that. I mean neither of you may want anything to do with me," said John.

"Well why don't we begin with your wants. What do you want, John? Do you want to spend your life with either of us?"

"After things fell apart with Cassilda I discovered how little I had prepared myself for love. Love isn't the easy thing people think it is. You have to have a big space within, like I was talking about before. It's not just the sacrifices that you're willing to make, it's not just the lust or the friendship—it's an inner bigness that lets the other person inside. I didn't have it for someone as great as Cassy."

"And now?" asked Cassilda.

"It's not that easy. When I found Michelle it was like that slave girl in the story. She was willing to do anything for me. Not in a self-deprecating way—in a 'let me be in your quest' way. I was smarter than Bion."

"Not much smarter. You left me here and I was kidnapped."

"Well at least I didn't sell you. Well I guess I did in a way. I was so stupid I might as well have given you to Chandra."

"So you want your little slave girl?" asked Cassilda.

"When I heard all you had done in order to get me back, you became my Witch Queen. You became every dark thing I'd always feared you would become, but now I was ready, I could handle it. I'm not scared of life. You remember my uncle Larry?"

"The one I went bungee jumping with?" asked Cassilda.

"Yeah. He was a timid little man who worked doing quality audits with hospitals until he had a heart attack. Then he came alive. He lives every day trying to ascend into the essence of life, to taste the juices of living. I've seen my own corpse, I understand my own death. I know I need you."

"You don't sound like you are coming to a decision," said Michelle.

"I can't. I've tried really hard, but I can't. If either of you were any less in my life, I would die. I am so glad that whatever seems to be waiting for me has put you both here in my home. This is like heaven after hell, day after night, but it will be over soon. I have traveled to Venusberg, but my time here is gone."

"Not necessarily," said Cassilda. "How much do you want heaven?"

"What do you mean?" asked John.

"When we were married you were afraid that I might share my love. I know it wasn't sex—there isn't a man alive who wouldn't come to bed with two beautiful women. It was love. You never believed when I told you that true love was not like gold or clay—to divide is not to take away. I have come to love Michelle. I loved her the moment I saw her on your mom's couch. She had gone through so much just because she loved you. At first I loved her because she loved you and had done so much for you, then I loved her because she was so capable of love, then I merely loved her," said Cassilda.

Michelle said, "I had never loved a woman before. I mean I had thought about the physical aspect and had been curious, but when Cassilda kissed me at Henry's, it was tender. You barely gave me a kiss at your mom's. Here I had gone through hell, and I didn't get love from you, but from my dark sister. I have never felt as close to anyone as I feel to Cassilda, except the way I feel to you."

"Are you sure, are you both sure? It has been so sudden," said John.

"John you really should have paid attention to Munchower's book. Like she says, time flows at different rates, and if you are at a place where the tide is flowing quickly, you must seize what you want," said Cassilda.

"And both of you still want me?" asked John.

"You are a complete shithead, aren't you, John? Hell, I took a bullet for your worthless hide, of course I want you," said Michelle.

"Then there is neither god nor man happier than I," said John, as he went forward to embrace the two women. They rocked back and forth in a long hug, and they cried. They held one another for a long time. Until Cassilda whispered in John's ear, "You know, I bet I am better at eating Michelle than you are."

"Bet you're not," said John.

"You may have to run more than one set of trials," said Michelle.

"We've got all night," said Cassilda.

Both Cassilda and John began undressing Michelle, first the shirt and pants, then the lacy red bra and matching panties. They picked her up and laid her down upon the bed. John, remembering an old custom from the days of his marriage, went into the laundry room and brought out candles that he began lighting around the room. He paused after the first one to come and kiss each of the women full on the mouth. Cassilda kissed Michelle for a while, but then began to work her way downward to the salty field of games. Michelle's initial soft cries told John that he would have to do his best, but for any man who has devoted his entire life to gaming, this should prove very easy. He undressed and joined them on the bed, stifling Michelle's cries of delight with his mouth. After a very few minutes Michelle began to shudder and her left leg to twitch as it always did before orgasm. He ran his hands over her breasts, roughly thumbing her large nipples. After the climax came and resided in a series of tiny aftershocks, Cassilda raised her head, her cheeks shiny with the jade water. John grabbed her by her hair and licked Michelle's juices from her cheeks and mouth, and then as if baited by that taste moved to the source, hot and wet from Cassilda's expert ministrations.

Almost the very instant that his tongue touched the hood's mystery, Michelle came again. John reckoned that this would prove the point of dispute, but did not stop his licking. Instead he added the first two fingers of his left hand. Michelle's cunt tightened on them and the flavor of her juices became acid squirting like a ruby red grapefruit. John began working on her ass with the pinkie of his right hand, but found his attention drawn to his penis as Cassilda began stroking it. He had to shift around so that she could use her mouth, if she wanted to. And much to John's relief she did. First with long sweeps of her tongue from the balls to the shaft, then teasingly just swallowing the knob, finally taking the whole length of the shaft in her mouth.

John's pinkie penetrated both sphincters. Michelle's ass was too tight for a lot of anal play, so lots of training in the future was indicated. Thank God, he had Cassy to count on for that. He could feel his fingers in Michelle's cunt and squeezed the warm flesh in between, timing each squeeze with the movement of Cassilda's mouth. But then in what was agony, Cassilda took her mouth away. John could hear her undressing, but didn't let his attention wander from the task at hand, which was rewarded noisily and spasmodically with another orgasm from Michelle.

Cassilda pulled on John's hips and he slipped away from Michelle only in time to be straddled by Cassilda. Cassy was so wet that she was able to take all of him in a single thrust. She must truly love Michelle. With delight upon delight John thought about how different the cunts of the two women were. Cassilda's was stronger, more experienced, more firm of grasp, whereas Michelle's was more delicate, almost virginal. That two such wonderful and amazing creatures should find love in each other was inevitable; that they had such a place for him despite his many weaknesses was miraculous.

Michelle left by way of the head of the bed and came around behind the now wildly thrusting Cassilda. She slipped one hand down to Cassilda's cunt and began stroking the front of it, mainly the clitoris, but occasionally John felt her fingertips at the opening where his cock was entering Cassilda. Michelle's other hand went to Cassilda's right breast, where she plucked the nipple in the way she enjoyed having her own nipples played with and aroused. Cassilda would turn her head half back and kiss Michelle in a clumsy fashion—hard to do anything with grace at this point. Michelle stopped playing with Cassilda's breast and took her hand to her own cunt.

The mutual sounds rose and blended and became almost harmonious. The weird threefold song raised and lowered and raised again and became a threefold crescendo that awakened the birds in the hackberry tree outside.

And after this the talk began, slowly at first, with laughs and sounds and gentle caresses, and the words began to bring a new world into being, a world for the three of them with no one of them in a privileged space, or more precisely a world in which any one of them would be an axis for a moment, ruler for a day, and where years of loneliness would leave, and years of blushingly great lusts would be assuaged, adventures could be had and dreams nourished, serious fantasies were discussed—not of a sexual sort but of long-term goals that each had lacked the courage to do before but had gained not just in the finding of one another but in the nature of finding one another, Cassilda foresaw her return to Austin in the spring, soon she would have to go back to Amarillo to fill out her job obligations, but she could teach here and tell the cards here and generally take advantage of the big writerly community, John could try long-term riskier projects like novels of his own instead of game tie-in books, Michelle was going to try for partner at the firm, they would travel, Michelle had always wanted to go to the theater festival at Edinburgh, and they could each help counsel the others at the death of their parents, they could get a bigger house, they could do anything.

John talked a great deal about getting back together with his younger brother, Matthew. Matthew and his wife used to play D&D with John and Cassilda. They had drifted apart a few years ago, about the time of John's divorce. Matthew's wife, Haidee, had been shot by someone robbing Matthew's used-book store. John had sunk too far in his orbit to do more than send flowers. He would reach out to Matthew. He had always felt "cheated" by Matthew. He always thought his other brothers, Saul and Paul, were lucky because they had each other. Twins. If Matthew had been earlier he could have been John's twin. He could have *saved* John from loneliness and boredom. He had never forgiven Matthew for not being his double. John felt that now he had substance of being to forgive him.

Words said at certain times affect the world directly. They felt and knew this.

The words were interrupted by periods of more lovemaking, and little naps and dreams that all flowed one into the other. This whole moment, this infinitely long and clear present, was blurring the distinctions of the objective and subjective universes of each—and secrets of their souls that they themselves could not speak, since they had not revealed to the Oracle, whispered themselves directly each to each to each.

About four in the morning, Michelle woke to the sound of John gently kissing Cassilda's neck. She said, "John, I think Henry is right, I think it will happen today. I see you under a sign of Z slash S and you look afraid, and I am afraid for you."

John and Cassilda listened to her concerns and held her and like adults who had been through so much strangeness knew not to tell her not to be worried, but to tell her not to be worried given the strength and safety of the moment.

"Did you know, John, that Michelle's middle name is Camilla? I think we should start calling her that so if you should happen to get excited and call one of us by the wrong name you won't be embarrassed."

"What happens if one of you gets excited and calls out 'John'?"

Camilla giggled and said, "That has already happened. We dealt with it."

24 Old Haunts and New

"Happy Halloween!" said Detective Anthony R. Blick. "What I'm about to tell you is just between you and me."

John had gone to the police station. It was odd how much more open and airy the rooms seemed when he wasn't being questioned.

"I understand," said John.

"After I overcame my neurosis that the Men In Black caused me, I checked up on all the things they had warned me away from as well on them. They're FBI agents, not very well regarded, and soon to be less so. The truth of the matter of Mason is that he did do some weird math stuff for the NSA. He quit on amicable terms, and no one would have noticed except that he went out of his way about a year ago to erase all of his records. If he hadn't tried to disappear, nobody would have noticed him at all. These three boys were trying to track him down and decided to start playing the Men In Black role. They seem somewhere down the line to have crossed the barrier between play and reality."

"Thanks for finding out. You know I owe them a debt."

"How so?"

"Well they broke my fear and power addictions. If they hadn't been so damn pathetic I wouldn't have broke out of my bowed-head approach to authority."

"Me, too."

"So what's the woods I'm still in?"

"I checked up as much as I could on Chandra Mason and didn't find much, and on the lecturer at the Lost Weekend and found out less. But Dr. Niles went into hiding after my investigation. Except for this." Blick held up a flyer.

Zandor Sinestro's Circus of Terror!
Frights like no other!
This Halloween Only.
Confront your greatest fears in Austin's best spookhouse.
We Are Seldom True Enough.

There was an address and a picture. The picture was of Dr. David R. Niles.

John recognized the address at the bottom of the flyer. It was in Austin's trendy warehouse district. It had been a used-book store managed by two poets, Chuck and Pat Taylor, and after that it had been a bar, a dojo, a gallery, and a coffeehouse. It had been one of his and Cassilda's favorite haunts.

"So?" said John.

"So I know you'll visit it. I just wanted to know if you wanted me to have a group of men ready to clean it out."

"No, I don't think so. I think I've got to have it out with Dr. Niles by myself. I think I've had to do that my whole life."

"I thought you might say that. I've been thinking for a while that this whole thing isn't my jurisdiction. I want you to have this."

Blick handed him a small blue medallion.

"My aunt Sadie gave this to me. It's a Saint Christopher medallion."

"Wasn't he downgraded a few years ago?" asked John.

"All right it's a Mr. Christopher medallion," said Blick.

"Thanks."

"You'll tell me everything, won't you?"

"I will tell you all."

The plan was simple. Henry would park his Explorer near the haunted house in the afternoon (nighttime would be hard to find a parking spot). John would ferry everyone down to the car about midnight and then would park his own car anywhere he could. Armed with Henry's .45, which Henry claimed had no paper trail at all, he would visit the haunted house. He also had a voice-activated tape recorder, a tiny camera (from a shop that banked on men's James Bond fantasies), and a hundred-dollar bill to bribe intermediaries to see Zandor Sinestro. The haunted house closed at midnight, and he would be the last person in line. He would force the encounter with Niles, and accept no nonsense.

Half of Austin was blocks away on Sixth Street. Drunk and sober adults milled in endless circles in front of bars and live music clubs, skeletons nodded at giant rabbits, gunslingers felt up witches, ghosts propositioned French maids, pirates shared joints with Marilyn Monroes, Caesars begged aspirin tablets from overweight Cleopatras, Shao-lin priests told Aggie jokes to Texas Rangers, and Shirley Temple told a space alien that she was ready to be abducted. The noise reached John standing in front of the Explorer watching the time and chatting with the family inside, when at 11:17 he saw Chandra Mason entering the front door of Zandor Sinestro's Circus of Terror! He ran the two blocks to the building. There were eight people in line ahead of him, mainly high school types hoping that the quick fear could lead to a quick grope. They proved uninterested in allowing John to move to the head of the line.

It was an eternity to get to the front. The doorkeeper looked like Charlie Manson and had the breath of the undead. John parted with his four dollars.

There was a tunnel inside mirrors in the shape of < >. John found that the floor moved slightly from right to left and back again. It was dark except for the green and purple strobe lights. He walked forward through the short tunnel and suddenly the floor rotated ninety degrees and he found himself facing a wooden door covered in cobwebs. It opened with an appropriate squeak and someone pushed John from behind into the room.

In the candlelit room was a murder scene. Someone had killed a beautiful woman with an ax, nearly beheading her. The gore-dripping ax lay on the table. Dr. Niles's voice said, "Watch your step, don't lose your head!"

"I need to talk to you!" yelled John.

Tiny plastic spiders began falling down from the ceiling and a spotlight revealed the next door. John jumped as the spiders hit the nape of his neck, and ran for the door.

The second chamber was lit by a mirror ball with a thousand points of light. It took John a minute to realize that there was someone in the room with him covered from head to toe in solid black. The someone fired up a chain saw and advanced toward John as another spotlight revealed another door.

In a gray-lit room covered in aluminum foil, two grays were

playing with a plasma ball. One of them picked up a huge syringe and began advancing toward John.

"I need to see Niles! It is an emergency!" he yelled. "Look, I'll pay."

The aliens looked at each other and pointed frantically toward the next door, which had been illuminated by the inevitable spotlight. John didn't know if they understood what he was saying, or if that's how they dealt with any nutcases that came through.

In the next room a machine shot out gusts of green flame while another machine shot hot air up from the floor. A recorded voice (not Niles's) said, "You've got to leave this room, our equipment isn't working right." The exit appeared and just as he was leaving a huge fireball billowed behind him.

Frankenstein's monster lay in the lab beyond. He was just rising from his slab surrounded by the sparking effect of two large Jacob's ladders. John ran up to him.

"I've got to see Sinestro. I'll pay for the chance."

The flesh golem looked him over, and then took the proffered bill.

"Dr. Niles is with another client, but you can wait."

The spotlight illuminated a door, but the green-faced monster took John's hand and led him to a section of wall. The wall became a door through some secret process and John began walking down a set of stairs. The monster closed the door behind John, and John found himself walking down a *dark* set of stairs.

He came to a narrow hallway. He felt his way along in the dark, and then it hit him. Everything that mattered to him in the world was up there on the ground, and he was pursuing this mystery—did he want to know so much?

About that time he heard angry screaming ahead.

He did want to know.

He surged forward. He ran straight into a door.

He felt for the knob, turned it, and saw the following scene: in a dimly lit room Dr. David R. Niles cowered behind a desk covered in maps; in front of the desk Chandra Mason held a gun in both hands pointed at Dr. Niles's head. Behind Chandra Mason the man from the thousand points of light room stood with a sock filled with something heavy—he had removed his facial covering, showing a sort of bullet-shaped head and greasy black hair. There was some kind of light source above the desk illuminating Dr. Niles, there seemed to be another vague source of illumination behind Chandra Mason, who was cursing Niles (apparently calling him a Ferringi?), the chain saw guy was about to hit Chandra, and Niles was mouthing something that John could not hear.

Chandra shot, and the man behind her hit her with the sap. She fell forward but he caught her before she hit the floor. Dr. Niles fell backward and a movie image of his face appeared on the wall behind the desk.

A door at the opposite end of the room opened and Dr. Niles walked in carrying a syringe. He plunged the syringe into Chandra's arm and said, "Take her to the tape room."

The chain saw guy began dragging her backward, the process causing her to lose her shoes.

John pulled his .45.

"Freeze."

Everyone froze.

"Good evening, Mr. Reynman. Please let Leggy take care of Mrs. Mason. I am glad to remain here as your hostage." He spread his arms out and wiggled each of his fingers, perhaps to show that he was unarmed. He then said, "We need to say as little as we can, please Mr. Reynman, every moment is crucial."

John motioned the man to drag Chandra away.

"May I adjust the lighting?" asked Dr. Niles.

"Very, very slowly. If the room goes black or white I will shoot."

"Very wise."

Niles crossed slowly to the desk, moved aside a map, and touched three buttons. The image of his silent mouthing face disappeared from the wall, and was replaced by a still image of a great god striding through the desert. In his left hand he held a scroll that was but partially written upon, and he read the scroll with half a glance and kept the other upon the horizon. In his right hand he held a key fashioned like the cross of the Egyptians. The general lighting in the room increased although John couldn't determine the source of the illumination. This was the same trick of lighting that the alien grays had used above. Behind the desk was a dummy dressed as Niles. Half of its face had been shot off—it had been quite convincing with the moving picture displayed on its face.

Niles picked up a rusty folding chair that had been hidden in the darkness and set it on one side of the desk. He took the dummy's seat.

"Please Mr. Reynman, sit, we have a brief time to talk."

"Why brief?"

"I have some self-created rules for such games. Limits can be a source of power, much as a blind man's blindness can cause him to sharpen his hearing."

"What does the figure behind your desk signify?"

"The ever-striding god is the self, which having remembered its divine potential seeks to find a place to be schooled in the divine. The horizon it seeks after is ever-receding, the lessons that make all clear appear on the scroll, but alas only one day at a time. In the course of its journey it finds keys that open doors in unexpected places. In fact the whole of its life is seen to be a key that fits a cosmic lock."

"Is that everything it means?"

237   **The Double: An Investigation**

"No. It can mean many, many things depending on when you look at it during your journey. One can step in the same stream but it is always new water that washes your feet."

"Did you know my father?"

"I met him in Recife, Brazil, and in Chicago. I gave him the key to the mysteries, which is the story of the origin of our little brotherhood. It begins you know with a man chasing a bus and seeing a girl. That man, Athanasius Kramden, founded the Society of Voyagers in 1923 in Chicago, Illinois. I took your father to the very spot of the founding on Clarke Street. The society seeks deathlessness, A-thanasia, by trying to be ever moving—in thought if not in actual buses. I gave him a solid gold bus token. I perceive you to be that token in an altered form."

"What's the real story of the Brotherhood of Travelers?"

"My personal favorite is that it was started by Boer farmers moving away north from Cape Town in the eighteenth century seeking to avoid the growing bureaucracy of the Dutch East India Company. They traveled by oxcart at night.

"Led by one Captain Albert Pike, they called their action trekking, which is an Afrikaans word from the Middle Dutch *trekken*, to pull along. They called themselves trekkers with the motto 'To boldly go where no Dutchman has gone before.' They drew mystic significance from the North, which is the place of Darkness in Masonry and the idea of 'darkest Africa.' "

"No, really, what is the origin?"

"Yage Tomas told me that the Lodge of Visitors was founded by Antonio da Ponte, the man who underbid Michelangelo for the Rialto Bridge in Venice in 1590. He stole a rare work on alchemy from the Vatican library called *The Azoth Messenger*, 'Azoth' coming from an Arabic word meaning mercury. The treatise being incomplete he traveled to the City of the Pillars in Arabia to learn the rest of the Secret. There he founded a brotherhood that oversees oases and hostels for the sake of the spiritual traveler. These oases are signs of places of rest where the traveler can contemplate his journey. Antonio da Ponte's motto was 'Better Living through Alchemy.' "

"You know that I can shoot you, don't you? I mean I've got a gun pointed right at you."

"You certainly do. I am quite aware of it."

"Then why don't you give me serious answers?"

"These are very serious answers. They may also be funny."

"But which is right?"

"They are all right. You can look them up in history books, and they are as true as any history recorded therein. Some say they were planted by the Society, others say they planted society."

"Is there an infinite number of these stories?"

"No, so far there are just twenty-four—if you were lucky enough to find that disk, you have them all. Even Mason's favorite."

"What was Mason's favorite?"

"I'm afraid I can't tell you. It's the file of pure math. He actually proved the existence of the Brotherhood. Thank God for that. Until he came along we didn't know for sure if we existed at all."

"Was Taylor Keziah Mason a member of the Brotherhood of Travelers?"

"He was a member in good standing until he broke into your house."

"Did breaking into my house violate some law?"

"We travel to see marvels, not to prevent them. Many times we find that the event we travel to see comes into being because of our presence, sometimes we become involved in it, but never are we to prevent it. The one ethical imperative is not to destroy another's destination."

"What are you doing to his wife?"

"Leggy is feeding her certain drugs and playing a little tape we prepared. She must believe that she has killed me, otherwise she would never be happy. Mason had used her terribly, and I find that sad. Let her remember him as a good man that she revenged. Soon the only images of him will be hers and yours, and since you didn't really know him, yours will fade. He will be reformed in her mind, becoming a good twin of his deceased self."

"Why must she think she has killed you?"

"Because I killed her husband. She figured it out. Not really very hard—who else knew him?"

"Why did you kill him?"

"Self-defense, he pulled a gun on me. This gun, in fact—I will show you very slowly."

Dr. Niles pulled a gun from the desk drawer and pushed it butt first to John.

"Why were you in my house?"

"I had followed Mason there. I knew that he was there to stop your Awakening. I wanted to talk him out of it. He pulled a gun on me, I shot him in your living room."

"How did he get into my house?"

"His father was a key cutter who belonged to a secret society that can get keys to any house in the world."

"What do you mean my Awakening?"

"Sometimes, under rare conditions, someone awakens to the possibilities of life, to the very state that makes you a member of the Brotherhood of Travelers, whether you know it or not. Mason had discovered that you were the one. He had developed a very precise formula for such things, a kind of psychohistory. When he found who and where, he decided to take your place. He had been through one Awakening and decided that if he went through two he could obtain a species of earthly immortality. The longevity and other powers that the Brotherhood has were very simply not enough for him. We tried to tell him he could not cheat the world the way he could cheat a computer simulation, but his greed overcame him."

"What happens to the Awakened?"

"They find their own destiny and change the world with it. We never know what Doors you may unlock, but your curiosity, your overwhelming urge to find out what happens next, will lead you to open Doors, and others will come through just as the Door I opened in Brazil allowed you to come through at the right time."

"What causes an Awakening?"

"Usually it takes a lifetime of certain sorts of training the imagination followed by an amazing, world-shattering event. In your case I would say finding a corpse that looked just like you in your house."

"But you didn't choose that, it wasn't your plan was it?"

"No, I thought I could talk Mason out of it. I would have got rid of the body, if I could have thought of any way to do it. I am sure that it has caused you a great deal of grief."

"But didn't that destroy another's destination?"

"Yes, I'm afraid so. That's why you have a decision now. As a new member of the Brotherhood you have the right to kill me for my crimes, or to pardon me. You must decide."

For a moment John wanted to kill him. All this cheap theater; Michelle's—eh Camilla's pain at being shot at; his mother—who was due for surgery in four days—sitting up there. Who was this man who played with people as though he were a god? No one would know. John felt sure that "Leggy" wasn't going to step out and intervene. But he had to know, he had to know in his mind who this man really was.

John stared hard at the man across the desk from him. He thought of all the things the last two weeks had brought. His vision of life, of its possibilities, of love and its many dimensions, of the number of mysteries that the cosmos might have for him, of the good he could do in the world, of Cassilda and Camilla, of all, and everything was so vast, he felt that he owed this man everything.

"I pardon you, but tell me, would all this have happened if you hadn't been around?"

John looked at Dr. Niles's eyes, which suddenly seemed very far away like stars, and then he realized that he was staring at two reflective points on the metal chair behind the desk, and that he had been staring at them for a very long time. He could not tell if Dr. Niles had vanished through some supernatural means, or if there had been a trick like the movie projector, or if in any real sense Dr. Niles had been there at all.

He got up, holstered his gun, and went to the stairs. In the world above was a whole new life, a life so abundant that he felt like a god striding toward an ever-receding horizon.

About the Author

Don Webb was born in Amarillo, Texas, and lives in the city of Austin. A prolific short-story writer, Don has had his work recommended in two or three "Year's Best" lists for the last fourteen years. His poetry, nonfiction, and weekly Internet column "Letters to the Fringe" are three of the principal ways he fails to make money writing. But he has also failed to make money in an astonishingly large number of small- and alternative-press appearances (two hundred plus). His fiction has been translated into eight languages. He denies that putting this—his first novel—under your pillow at night will bring strange Dreams.